PANAMA'S
CANAL

PANAMA'S CANAL

BY CARL R. OLIVER

FRANKLIN WATTS
New York · London · Toronto · Sydney · 1990

All photographs courtesy of Carl R. Oliver and: U.S. Military Academy: p. 15;
National Archives: pp. 20 top, 27, 32, 35, 40, 42, 43 top, 45, 46 bottom, 49, 63,
81; Library of Congress: pp. 20 bottom, 29 top, 37; General Electric: p. 47.

Library of Congress Cataloging-in-Publication Data

Oliver, Carl R.

Panama's Canal / by Carl R. Oliver.

p.   cm.

Contents: Includes bibliographical references.

Summary: An overview of the history of the Panama Canal, from its
construction through the 1977 agreement turning over sovereignty to
the Panamanian government to its possibilities for the future.

ISBN 0-531-10958-5

1. Panama Canal (Panama)—History—Juvenile literature.
[1. Panama Canal (Panama)—History.]   I. Title.

F1569.C2043   1990

972.87'5—dc20   90-34273   CIP   AC

CONTENTS

1

Sovereignty . . . Won?

9

2

Sovereignty . . . Lost?

19

3

Proud Workers

26

4

Why the Canal Succeeded

36

5

A Nation Divided

48

6

Special People

58

7

The Challenge

72

8

Winds of Change

78

Appendix

86

Source Notes

90

Bibliography

93

Index

94

PANAMA'S CANAL

Chapter 1

SOVEREIGNTY...
WON?

On January 7, 1964, American students gathered at the flagpole in front of Balboa High School, Panama Canal Zone. They raised the flag of the United States of America. The students knew this would anger Panamanians.

Americans had flown the Stars and Stripes in the Panama Canal Zone for sixty years. Now a new international treaty, signed by the United States and the Republic of Panama, changed the rules. The treaty made it illegal to fly the flag of the United States in the Panama Canal Zone unless the flag of Panama flew right alongside it.

There was nothing wrong with both governments agreeing to "change the rules." But to these students, who lived beside the famous canal, flying America's flag was important. They felt proud that America had built the Panama Canal, an engineering marvel some people have labeled the "Eighth Wonder of the World."

To the Panamanians, flying Panama's flag was equally important. Panamanians gathered in the streets of Panama City to protest the American flag raising. They felt proud that the canal crossed their homeland, Panama. They had deep-rooted feelings about their right and duty to make sure Panama's national flag flew in the Panama Canal Zone.

The demonstrations became riots. By January 12, when the riots finally ceased, twenty Panamanians and four Americans lay dead—all because American students flew Old Glory at their school.

To understand how this tragedy could happen is to understand a great deal about Panamanians and other peoples who call Central Amer-

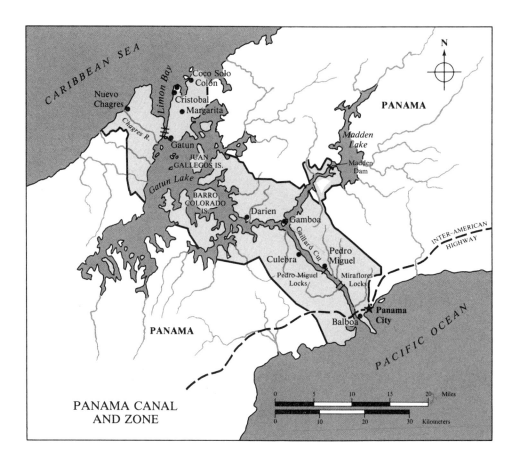

Caribbean Sea

PANAMA CANAL
AND ZONE

ica their home. Both sides felt motivated by well-deserved love for the Panama Canal.

Construction of the Panama Canal across the tropical mountains of Panama was truly an astonishing feat. From the start, this canal played an important role in world affairs. Through the 1990s and into the twenty-first century, the canal will continue to attract much attention from many nations of the world because the Panama Canal is far more than an engineering marvel that carries ships between the Atlantic and Pacific oceans. It's a psychological symbol, a political prize, an economic necessity, and a military target. Events at the Panama Canal affect the commerce of every nation in the world.

What makes the next decade particularly important is that the canal will change ownership. The United States, which built the canal, will give it to Panama. The deadline is noon on December 31, 1999. Some Panamanians say that's too late. They want the canal handed over sooner.

They seem unable to rest until the world recognizes the canal as exclusively Panama's.

The transfer of ownership is not simple. The United States and Panama both have many questions to answer and many decisions to make. Is it possible for the United States to totally abandon the canal? Would Panama really want the United States to leave completely?

The United States has military bases in Panama to protect the canal. By treaty, U.S. military personnel must leave those bases by December 31, 1999. There are obvious questions: Will the departure of U.S. soldiers invite attack? Can Panama's small *Fuerza Pública*—more police force than army—defend the canal? If not, who will?

Who can predict what nation might attack the canal or for what reason? During World War II, Japan built submarines to launch special airplanes to bomb the canal. Not since then has any nation undertaken to attack the Panama Canal. But the political instability of Central American nations is well known. In 1969, a shooting war broke out between El Salvador and Honduras that was linked to high emotions caused by a three-game soccer match between teams of the two countries.

Another Central American neighbor, Nicaragua, built military airfields big enough to launch jet bombers that could reach the canal. Cuba also attempted to build a major airfield on the Caribbean island of Grenada, close enough to the canal that air attacks would be possible.

There are not-so-obvious questions, too. When the United States leaves, Panamanians working on U.S. military bases will lose their jobs. Will they be able to find new employers quickly? Panama already has high unemployment—more citizens than jobs. When the United States turns over the canal and Panama takes charge, Panamanians working for the canal will find they have a new boss with new rules. How will they adjust?

The Panama Canal could fail financially. During some years, the United States spent more money to operate the canal than tolls brought in. Panama, a small nation, does not have money to spare. In fact, Panama depends on the profits from the canal for normal government functions. And Panama depends on the canal to attract businesses that produce jobs and incomes for its people. Failure of the Panama Canal would be a catastrophic financial disaster for Panama.

An unanswerable question is how much the Panama Canal has contributed to the prosperity, peace, and stability of Latin American nations. What will be its role in the future? In United States hands, the canal has offered every nation equal access at equal rates. Will Panama give some nations special rates? Will Panama tell some nations their ships cannot use the canal?

Recently, Panama Canal employees were uncomfortably in the middle of an official dispute between Panama and the United States. For the United States, the problem was how to stop large shipments of illegal drugs. United States grand juries indicted General Manuel Antonio Noriega, the former leader of Panama and commander of its *Guardia Nacional,* on charges that Noriega shipped illegal drugs into the United States for personal profit.

To stop these shipments, the United States cut off money to Noriega's government by "freezing" a large amount of Panama's money that was in American banks—the place where money collected by the Panama Canal is kept. Panama could not get it out. This included Panama's share of tolls, and taxes the canal withheld from the paychecks of Panamanian employees. Panama reacted by going to court to collect "unpaid" taxes by seizing canal employees' homes and cars.

This did not make the chairman of the Panama Canal's Board of Directors, William R. Gianelli, happy. He wanted both the U.S. and Panamanian governments to keep the canal and its employees out of political disputes. Gianelli told employees that the Panama Canal would pay them salaries while they were in court, pay them for lost homes and cars, and provide temporary housing if Panama took their homes.[1]

Americans employed by the canal felt the chill, too. A canal pilot who has loved the canal and life in Panama found himself discouraged. "For the time being, I am still in Panama. . . . The political situation is fragile here. . . . I could not live on what I would draw in retirement and things are still not that bad here, so I am not beating the bushes too hard [yet] looking for another job."[2]

What will the canal contribute to Panama and to Panama's economy? Will the United States want to use the canal in moments of military crisis? Will it be able to?

In 1962, the United States did use the canal to rush warships to meet the Cuban missile crisis. United States reconnaissance had discovered the Soviets building missile bases in Cuba. President John F. Kennedy ordered U.S. military forces to blockade Cuba to stop military equipment from arriving there. On November 5, 1962, twenty-three Navy ships arrived at the Pacific end of the Panama Canal and they crossed to the Atlantic end within twelve hours.

Ships were important to world commerce when the canal was built nearly a century ago. Are ships more important today? In years past, nations sought to be independent. They tried to produce everything they needed. Today "interdependence" means closer relations among nations. They tend to depend on each other, each specializing in products it makes best.

For example, a few years ago it was possible to buy a car completely made in America. Today, every American car contains parts made elsewhere. Fenders made in Japan travel to the United States by ship. If the fenders are bound for assembly plants in the eastern part of the country, the ship is likely to sail though the Panama Canal. Japan sends complete cars through the canal to the United States too, almost two million tons each year.

Let's look back in time to find out why the Panama Canal was built and how the United States got involved. In addition to Panama, three nations played major roles. In the 1500s, Spain wanted a canal but dared not build one. In the 1880s, France dared to try, but after twenty years of work declared its effort a failure. In 1904, the United States undertook construction and succeeded.

Christopher Columbus won fame as the first European to search for a waterway that would carry his ships farther west, through the continents he had discovered, to East Asia. In 1502, he explored Limon Bay, which now is the Atlantic entrance to the canal. He talked to Indians using sign language. We think they tried to tell Columbus the land at Panama was narrow and that another ocean lay just a short distance away. Columbus did not leave his ship to explore the jungle shores, so he never saw the Pacific Ocean.

Vasco Nuñez de Balboa did. In 1513, the Indians led Balboa and 190 Spanish shipmates on a hike across Panama, and Balboa "discovered" what he called the "Great South Sea." We call it the Pacific Ocean.

The discovery caused great excitement in Europe. Two mighty oceans separated by just a narrow piece of land. Europeans dreamed of a canal to join them, and within sixty years after Columbus's visit had considered five different routes the canal could take.

The trouble was that people living far away imagined a canal could be built, but people living in the tropical jungle of Panama knew it could not. From Europe, Spain's King Charles V sent orders in 1534 to his governor at Panama: Survey a route for a canal to be built by Spain. From Panama, the governor replied with dismay, "All the gold in the world would not suffice for its execution."[3]

The problem was that 50 miles (80.5 km) of land were covered with a dense jungle rain forest that stretched over the continental divide, mountains dividing the land so rain falling on one side created rivers flowing into the Atlantic while rain falling on the other flowed into the Pacific.

It would be more than 300 years before anyone was brave (or foolish) enough to seriously attempt building a canal across Panama. France was a mighty nation, a world power, and its hero, Count Ferdinand de Lesseps, had used modern machines to build a canal more than 100 miles (161 km) long across the sand at Suez. The French dreamed of de Lesseps building a canal at Panama.

De Lesseps found out what Panama was like:

There are next to no roads, and what few exist are very badly kept. Excepting these, the only means of transportation are the rivers, and many of these are very difficult to travel by boat because they have rapids which the Indian avoids by carrying his canoe overland.

The climate is a very hot one. It rains often for six months of the year, the annual rainfall at Panama exceeding ten feet.

It is not surprising that with such a high temperature and so heavy a rainfall the vegetation grows rapidly. Thus the plant life of the isthmus is very abundant and the virgin forests with their gigantic cactus and cocoa trees and their undergrowth—across which the native cuts a path with his axe or knife—form a tangled network.

It would almost seem as if all the poisonous snakes, spiders, and scorpions of Noah's ark had been emptied here, the country swarming with serpents whose bite is fatal, monstrous spiders, scorpions, and jaguars.[4]

After eight years of talking about a Panama Canal, French scientists took a vote at a conference in May 1879. Count de Lesseps was there, voted for the canal, and announced, "And I have agreed to be in charge of the enterprise!"[5] Others applauded him.

Count de Lesseps had decided "the Panama [Canal] will be easier to make, easier to complete, and easier to keep up than the Suez Canal."[6]

How wrong he was!

A French company's state-of-the-art bucket excavator digging
the canal channel in Panama during the late nineteenth century

Frenchmen worked at building a Panama Canal for twenty years.
They dug some trenches, but nothing that looked like a canal. They had
mighty digging machinery. But Count de Lesseps—once known as "The
Great Frenchman"—came to be called "The Great Undertaker" because
yellow fever and malaria killed many French workmen. Friends were
strongly affected by watching the agony of their dying companions.

Jules Isidore Dingler, for example, arrived in Panama on March 1,
1883, to direct construction of the canal. In the autumn, he brought his
wife, son, daughter, and his daughter's fiancé to Panama.

In January 1884, the eighteen-year-old daughter died of yellow
fever.

In February 1884, the son died of yellow fever.

Within weeks, the fiancé died of yellow fever.

At year's end, December 31, 1884, the wife died of yellow fever.

Eight months later, in August 1885, Jules Isidore Dingler gave up, quit his job, and returned to France.

Stories of sickness in Panama reached France and discouraged people from investing more money in the canal project. Finally, the French could not raise enough money to continue paying for work to be done. They gave up. They left their digging machines and railroad cars wherever they happened to be along the canal route. Jungle bushes and trees grew over the abandoned tools.

But the people who lived in Panama had changed. Now they dreamed that a canal *could* be built by someone. If mighty France had failed despite years of trying, who could possibly succeed? Not the Panamanians themselves. They saw only one hope: the United States.

Panamanians thought the United States was a "colossal" nation with enough money and enough brains to succeed where France had failed. Panama hoped to entice the United States to try.

And that's what happened. Colombian Minister Dr. Tomás Herrán signed a treaty on January 22, 1903, and the United States Senate voted in February to ratify it. It was an agreement whereby the United States would build a canal across Panama. But the treaty also had to be approved by the government of Colombia, which owned Panama at the time. The *New York World*—Joseph Pulitzer's newspaper known for its yellow journalism and sensationalism—reported trouble:

Advices received [in Washington, D.C.] daily indicate great opposition to the canal treaty at Bogotá [Colombia]. Its defeat seems probable for two reasons:

> *1. The greed of the Colombian Government, which insists on a largely increased payment for the property and concession.*
> *2. The fact that certain factions have worked themselves into a frenzy over the alleged relinquishment of sovereignty to lands necessary for building the canal.*

Information also has reached [Washington] that the State of Panama, which embraces all the proposed canal zone, stands ready to secede from Colombia and enter into a canal treaty [directly] with the United States. . . . The State of Panama will secede [from Colombia] if the Colombian

[16]

Congress fails to ratify the canal treaty. A republican form of government will be organized. This plan is said to be easy . . . as not more than 100 Colombian soldiers are stationed in the State of Panama.

The citizens of Panama propose, after seceding, to make a treaty . . . giving [the United States] the equivalent of absolute sovereignty over the canal zone. The city of Panama alone will be excepted from this zone, and the United States will be given police and sanitary control there. The jurisdiction of [the United States] over the zone will be regarded as supreme.[7]

Curiously, what the *World* predicted was exactly what happened. Colombia rejected the canal treaty on August 12, 1903. Two months passed. Then the United States Navy sent orders to ships in its Pacific Ocean Squadron on October 15: begin sailing southward. On October 30, the Navy ordered its warship the U.S.S. *Nashville* to leave Kingston, Jamaica, and steam to Limon Bay.

Colombia was not asleep. Trouble was brewing in Panama, so Bogotá dispatched 500 soldiers to Limon Bay aboard its navy gunboat *Cartagena*.

The *Nashville* arrived about 5:30 P.M. on November 2.

The *Cartagena* arrived close to midnight.

Troops stayed aboard both ships until daybreak. Then Colombian soldiers went ashore into the town of Colón. They were warmly greeted by Panamanians, who offered a fast, one-car special train to whisk the Colombian commander, General Juan Tobar, and his deputy and personal staff across the isthmus to comfortable Panama City. They promised a large train to take the general's 500 soldiers to Panama City right behind him, just as quickly as the necessary locomotives and rail cars could be assembled.

General Tobar accepted the offer. Evening found him in Panama City . . . and his 500 soldiers still waiting on the other side of the isthmus for their train. It was a trick, of course. The Panamanians threw General Tobar in jail and declared Panama an independent nation.

At dawn the next day, the American commander of the *Nashville* sent orders to the railroad not to move any military troops anywhere. The Colombian colonel who had been left in command of the 500 soldiers learned his general was in jail. Furious, the colonel ordered Colombian soldiers to surround the railroad station, and he threatened to burn the town of Colón to the ground and kill every American in sight.

The *Nashville* aimed its guns at the soldiers and the *Cartagena.*

Surprisingly, the *Cartagena* now raised anchor and steamed out of port, leaving Colombian soldiers with no large naval guns. For two days, tension remained high, but there was no fighting.

On November 5, at about 6:20 P.M., a ship was faintly seen on the horizon. It was the U.S. Navy warship *Dixie* arriving from Cuba.

Panamanians told the Colombian colonel that there were 5,000 American soldiers arriving in Panama. They offered the colonel $8,000 in gold to leave and take his soldiers with him.

The colonel accepted. A Royal Mail steamer, *Orinoco,* carried them away at 7:35 P.M.

Although 5,000 American troops never did arrive in Panama, eight more U.S. Navy ships did. With this visible support, the new Panamanian leaders sent a telegram to Washington, D.C., appointing an envoy to negotiate with the United States to build a Panama Canal.

Panamanians were proud. They had won their sovereignty—or so it seemed at the time.

Chapter 2

SOVEREIGNTY... LOST?

Five years before Panama declared independence, the United States had sent its battleship *Maine* to Havana, Cuba, to "show the flag," a traditional way to signal that America's political and economic interests would be affected by events in a foreign country.

This was precipitated by Spain claiming Cuba as its colony. For three years, however, Cubans had struggled to oust Spain and win independence.

On February 15, 1898, an explosion sank the *Maine* in Havana harbor and killed 260 American sailors. In the days that followed, Spanish investigators concluded that the explosion appeared to have originated on board the *Maine* and that it was accidental. American investigators concluded that a mine had exploded under the ship, but could not determine who had placed it there. Certain U.S. newspapers concluded that the explosion was an "enemy action." They coined the slogan, "Remember the *Maine*, to h—— with Spain!" and agitated for the United States to send its Army and Navy to help Cuban rebels.

On March 19, the U.S. Navy ordered its battleship *Oregon* to leave San Francisco, beginning what newspapers called "The Race of the *Oregon*." Built in 1891, the *Oregon* was a modern battleship able to steam at 15 knots. The *Oregon* steamed toward Cuba. . . .

Congress declared Cuba had a right to independence, demanded Spain withdraw military forces from Cuba, and authorized the Army and Navy to force Spain to withdraw.

The *Oregon* steamed toward Cuba. . . .

Battleship *Maine* after
wreckage was raised
from the bottom of
Havana harbor
in 1912

The battleship *Oregon*
required sixty-seven
days to race around
Cape Horn from San
Francisco to Cuba.

In response to Congress, Spain declared war on the United States on April 24, 1898.

The *Oregon* steamed toward Cuba. . . .

In turn, the United States declared war on Spain the following day.

The *Oregon* steamed toward Cuba . . . down the west coast of the United States, down the west coast of South America, around Cape Horn, and up the east coast of South America.

On May 24, after sixty-seven days at sea, the *Oregon* arrived at Cuba.[1]

If a canal had been built, the *Oregon* would have reached Cuba far sooner. People who wanted a canal were not reluctant to point out that fact.

If the United States would build a canal, the U.S. Navy could quickly concentrate warships in either ocean to defend America. Ships could haul cargo quickly and easily between the east and west coasts of the United States. And no other nation would have a chance to build a canal where they could charge U.S. ships a great deal to sail through.

Some people say a canal could be built anywhere. "Given the time, manpower, equipment, and money, a canal to join the Atlantic and Pacific oceans could be constructed anywhere from the frigid northern border of Canada to Tierra del Fuego [at the southernmost tip of South America]."[2]

In 1811, Baron Alexander von Humboldt of Germany said a canal already had been built in Colombia:

> [T]he small ravine de la Raspadura unites the neighboring sources of the . . . San Juan [river] and the small river Quito [a tributary of the Atrato River]. . . . A monk of great activity, curé of the village of Novita, employed his parishioners to dig a small canal in the ravine de la Raspadura by means of which, when the rains are abundant, canoes loaded with cacao pass from sea to sea. This . . . has existed since 1788, unknown in Europe. The small canal of Raspadura unites on the coast of the two oceans two points 75 leagues [about 225 miles (362 km)] distant from one another.[3]

Von Humboldt said he found the canal during five years of travel through Latin America. No one else ever found any sign of it. The Atrato and San Juan are wonderful rivers, but a canal to join them would be 95 miles (152.8 km) long and cross the continental divide mountains at 932 feet (284 m) above sea level.

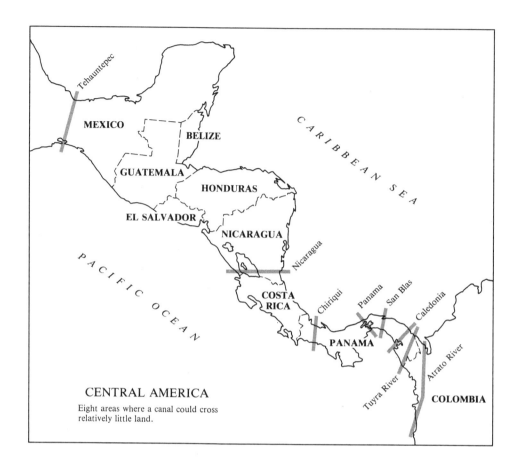

CENTRAL AMERICA

Eight areas where a canal could cross relatively little land.

Practical minds decided two locations for a canal were best: Nicaragua or Panama. The argument over which to build on became known as "The Battle of the Routes." It was heard in the U.S. Senate during the first six months of 1902.

The leader of the arguments favoring Nicaragua was Alabama Senator John Tyler Morgan, who had earned a reputation for being an honest man. The star attraction was natural Lake Nicaragua, 100 miles (161 km) long by 40 miles (64 km) wide, which could be a major leg of the canal. The mountains to be crossed were low, only 153 feet (46.6 m) above sea level, and because Nicaragua is close to the United States, ships could save hundreds of miles between U.S. coasts.

The leader of the arguments favoring a route across Panama was President Theodore Roosevelt, who trusted engineers' advice that Panama was a more practical place to build. This canal would be only 50 miles

(80.5 km) long and cross the mountains at a low saddle 340 feet (103.6 m) above sea level.

Arguments in favor of Nicaragua were very strong. Meanwhile . . .

On May 8, 1902, at 7:52 A.M., volcano Mount Pelée erupted and destroyed the city and people of St. Pierre on the island of Martinique in the Caribbean, almost 1,500 miles (2,415 km) from Nicaragua.

On May 14, reports arrived of another volcanic eruption: Momotombo in Nicaragua, 100 miles (161 km) from the proposed Nicaragua canal.

On May 20, Mount Pelée erupted explosively again and another volcano erupted on the island of St. Vincent, south of Martinique.

Senators were told not to worry, that Nicaragua had no volcanoes posing a genuine threat to a canal. Someone said stories about volcanoes erupting in Nicaragua were totally untrue.

On June 16, a leaflet was delivered to the office of every U.S. senator bearing official evidence to the contrary: an official Nicaraguan postage stamp that pictured a train on a wharf in Nicaragua with volcano Momotombo in smoking eruption behind the train. The leaflet said: "Postage Stamp of the Republic of Nicaragua. An official witness of the volcanic activity on the Isthmus of Nicaragua."[4]

The stamps were sent by Philippe Bunau-Varilla, who was in Washington, D.C., to encourage the United States to buy rights to build a canal across Panama. Bunau-Varilla was an engineer who had worked on the canal for France. After the French effort failed, he continued to urge construction of a canal. Some historians suspect he was a schemer trying to make money. Others report he was inspired by the dream of a canal. Historians agree he was the key person who arranged for France and Panama to sell rights to the United States to build a canal, and that he arranged favorable terms United States politicians would accept.

Three days after the stamps arrived, the Senate voted to build a Panama Canal.

As envoy of Panama, Bunau-Varilla negotiated the Panama Canal Treaty with the United States. Key points included these:

- The canal would be built in a zone ten miles wide that crossed Panama from coast to coast.
- Within the zone, the United States would hold all sovereign rights, power, and authority.

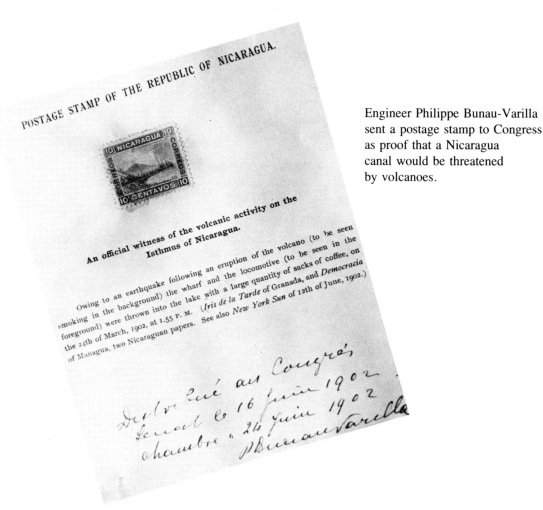

POSTAGE STAMP OF THE REPUBLIC OF NICARAGUA.

An official witness of the volcanic activity on the
Isthmus of Nicaragua.

Owing to an earthquake following an eruption of the volcano (to be seen
smoking in the background) the wharf and the locomotive (to be seen in the
foreground) were thrown into the lake with a large quantity of sacks of coffee, on
the 24th of March, 1902, at 1.55 P. M. (*Iris de la Tarde* of Granada, and *Democracia*
of Managua, two Nicaraguan papers. See also *New York Sun* of 12th of June, 1902.)

Engineer Philippe Bunau-Varilla
sent a postage stamp to Congress
as proof that a Nicaragua
canal would be threatened
by volcanoes.

- The United States could take control of any other Panama land
  or water needed to build, operate, protect, or maintain the canal.
- The United States would pay $10 million to Panama once, then
  $250,000 each year, and protect Panama from enemies.
- The treaty would last in "perpetuity"—for time without end.

Some Panamanians didn't like the treaty, but every town council approved it. In May 1904, the United States took charge in the Canal Zone.

Evidence shows that most Panamanians seemed happy with the arrangement in its earliest years. In 1906, President Theodore Roosevelt arrived in the Panama Canal Zone to personally inspect canal construction. (This was the first time any president had set foot on foreign soil.) American crews had been hard at work for two years—steam shovels were digging the canal channel—but much work remained to be done and completion of the canal still lay many years in the future. In honor of President Roosevelt's arrival, President Manuel Amador gave a speech on November 14, 1906. Dr. Amador was very happy, very positive, very encouraging. He said:

A rare alliance this, Mr. Roosevelt . . . the great Colossus of the North, with its immense riches, unlimited credit, its vast store of knowledge, and numerous elements that contribute to make it the only entity capable of successfully carrying on such a great enterprise, with the small and the youngest republic of America, owner of the land, which she gladly lends for the work . . .[5]

But evidence also shows that some Panamanians had serious misgivings about the arrangement. Panamanians were proud of the canal, but unhappy over who was sovereign in the Panama Canal Zone. This one issue became the most important Panama Canal controversy through the passing years. A sovereign is the supreme ruler, servant to no one. For a nation, sovereignty is status as a completely independent nation, master of its own destiny.

In 1919, Panamanians sent Resolution No. 25 to the U.S. Senate:

Whereas a motion has been made in the Senate of the United States to change the name of the canal from Panama to Roosevelt;

While that well-deserving citizen, who was a great friend of our Republic, is worthy of that honor and higher ones, the Panamanian people would feel genuine patriotic displeasure at having the greatest product of man's effort stripped of the name of this country, by which it is known throughout the world; and

The least that can be asked by the country which allowed itself to be torn up for the good of the world is that its name stay linked with the grand undertaking: Therefore

The National Assembly of Panama resolves, *To make known to the Senate and people of the United States its earnest and express desire that the name of Panama Canal continue to be given to the waterway which connects across the Isthmus the two largest oceans, and at the same time make known the pleasure with which the Panamanian people would join in any other way of glorifying the name of Roosevelt.*[6]

In Resolution No. 25, Panama acknowledged the reality that it was powerless to name the canal and recognized that the United States—a foreign nation—held the supreme, absolute, paramount, sovereign power to name the canal anything it chose.

What had Panama's envoy, Philippe Bunau-Varilla, signed away to the Americans? What had he sold? Was part of Panama's sovereignty lost?

Chapter 3

PROUD WORKERS

The people who built the Panama Canal were divided into two classes. Laborers were paid in silver coin and called silver employees. Most of these workers were blacks recruited in the tropics. Craftsmen and executives were paid in gold coin and called gold employees. Most of these people were whites recruited in the United States.

There were gold towns and silver towns, gold rest rooms and silver rest rooms, gold restaurants and silver restaurants. It was racial discrimination.

"The division of labor between the two classes of employees," said an official canal report, "is a matter of long custom in tropical countries, and Panama Canal practice conforms to this general custom."[1]

It *could* be explained as facilities of high quality for the rich, of lesser quality for the poor. Canal management sometimes explained that the goal was to give each group the same living conditions it enjoyed in its native land.

It *could* be explained medically. The famous Dr. William Crawford Gorgas, chief physician during canal construction days, said that keeping whites from the United States apart from blacks native to the tropics reduced chances that one group would infect the other with a disease not native to its homeland, for which no immunity had been built up.

Despite the discrimination, people who built the canal felt pride so strong that *New York World* reporter Earl Harding called it "canalitis." He said, "Once you have touched Panama, you never lose the infection."[2]

Left: Silver employees
gather for a meal at the
construction kitchen.
Each man bought a plate,
cup, and spoon out of
the first day's wages.
Above: Dr. William
Crawford Gorgas

President Theodore Roosevelt also noticed canal employees' unusually strong pride, calling it "a spirit which elsewhere has been found only in a few victorious armies."[3]

The builders shared a captivating dream—*the* greatest dream of the age: a canal that would join together the world's two largest, deepest oceans. Silver employee J. E. LeCurrieux captured the mood when he wrote, "I, the undersigned, was in all of this great mystery . . . of connecting the two oceans together."[4]

The flavor of canal construction life appears in essays silver employees wrote years later.

LeCurrieux remembered a rigid medical examination before boarding the ship. After arriving in Colón, the men rode trains to various camps along the canal route. "Then we were taken to a kitchen and each of us [was] given one plate, one cup, one spoon, and a meal. Then those utensils were ours—the price to be taken out of our first pay. We were given a meal ticket valued at thirty cents that entitled each one of us to an evening meal and a ticket blank for our coffee the next morning and a midday meal, also a ticket which entitled each one of us to a shelter for the night."

Leslie Carmichael remembered,

While the gang [was] laying rails, we were short of drinking water. I was among the men sent to get a supply to be taken from the Chagres River. We were to use a pump car to carry the eight 5-gallon [19 l] cans and a 50-gallon [189 l] barrel. On our way we were followed by about ten lions running behind the car. They were getting closer and closer to us. While holding the barrel with one hand to steady it, I took one of the cans and used it to scare them off by hitting it to make a noise that drove them away.

Water to drink was very hard to get to supply so [many] men. There were times when we would lie on our stomach and drink whatever water [was] in sight to quench our thirst. By drinking water that way, a lot of the workers died from black fever and yellow fever.

Edgar Llewellyn Simmons

. . . got a job in the powder gang at Gatun, where all those huge trees were blown up with dynamite. After blowing up the trees, we had axe men cut holes in each tree. Some trees had up to fifteen holes or more. After the holes were cut, two or three sticks of dynamite were placed in

[28]

Early symptoms of
''canalitis.'' Boys
growing up in the canal
construction town
play with a home-built
toy Bucyrus steam
shovel in 1906.

Canal commissary
store in June 1915,
with separate
entrances for
gold and silver
employees

the holes, with a cap and coil about eighteen inches long and covered with mud.

After the 5:15 passenger train passed for Panama [City], we started lighting. Some of us had up to sixty-five or seventy-two holes to light and find our way out. Nine of us start out, each one with two sticks of fire in our hands, running and lighting [and] trying to clear ourselves before the first set begin bursting on us. Then it's like Hell. Excuse me for this assertion, but it's a fact.

On one occasion, myself and a fellow called Stanley Shockness had to jump in the river that ran down to the old pump station and hide ourselves under the wild mango roots until all was over.

After this, the regular gang would pile it up. Then, days or weeks after, we—the same lighters—would go around with crude oil and a long brass torch, spilling the oil all over the heap, then applying our torch.

Sir, another Hell roared again.

Albert Peters worked as a barge diver.

There was one operator, one oiler, and four divers on each barge. It wasn't necessary for all four divers to go overboard at the same time. As the shift was eight hours, we made an agreement for each man to dive two hours only, unless there was something very heavy for him to bring up, then everybody would give a hand.

Well, this particular day was pay day. The pay car was on the other side of the bank, paying. The rule was, if you don't get your pay while the pay car is on the road, you couldn't get it until it has finished, and then you get it at the Administration Building in Ancon.

The other men got their pay. They went across the bridge which was about one hundred yards down the cut. It was my two-hour shift, and that old pump had me overboard every three or four minutes. Rock and grass choking it. Every time I came up, I watched the car on the opposite bank.

All of a sudden, I heard it blow its whistle before going. I ran out on the end of the barge and waved my hands and hollered. They saw me and stopped.

I grabbed my brass check [identification badge], put it in my cap, and slid on a wire overboard, swam across, then had to climb a 40-foot [12 m] muddy hill. When I got to the top, the pay car was about twenty feet in front of me.

I was so exhausted the policeman took my cap and helped me into the car. There was my pay in front of me on the counter. I was as naked as I came into this world, except for my cap and [money], and I was the last one paid at that [location] that day.

James A. Williams worked as a kitchen helper on the bank of the Chagres River.

I began to get fever. One morning the doctor, making his usual visit to the kitchen, felt my pulse. He said to me, "You are going to be sick, boy. Go right over to the sick camp and tell the clerk to write you up to the hospital. Right away."

He further asked me, "Are you a God-fearing man?"

I replied yes.

He said to me, "You are going to die."

It was near time for the midday train, and the doctor ran over to the sick camp and [helped] to write up the necessary papers and I was placed on the train to the Ancon hospital.

I was placed on a bed on the train to the hospital all the way, and when the train arrived in the Panama station there were many horse-drawn ambulances waiting to receive the patients. We arrived in the big Ward 30 and a very pleasant American nurse was right on the job and started to feel the pulses and assigned each patient to a different bed.

When she came to me and took my hand, she appeared to be frightened and she called to the orderly and said to him, "Do not put this patient under the shower. Give him a bed bath."

I wondered to myself, what is this bed bath?

[An orderly, Norman] Piercy, placed a heavy waterproof blanket in the bed, and two bucketfuls of heavy, crushed ice, and several buckets of water. And he had not even the courtesy as to consult me, but stripped me naked and threw me in that cold, deadly water.

To be truthful, I thought I could not any longer live. However, he gave me a thorough bathing and took me out and dried me with a towel and placed me in a white, clean bed. I felt cool for a moment, but still was fretting over the iced bath as I had never heard or seen anything of that kind before.

The next shock I had while I felt a little thirsty. When I saw someone coming, a nurse, with a glass of water, I felt glad as I thought it was some cool water which I felt so much the need of. And the kindly nurse handed it to me and said, "Drink it."

So, thirsty for a drink of water, I hurried and as it reached my lips

Horse-drawn ambulance at Ancon Hospital during canal construction days

it was down into my stomach. I tell you! I had never before tasted anything so terribly bitter. I was always hearing about quinine, but I thought it was something tasty and nice. And every two hours I was dosed with that bitter liquid, night and day, and instead of getting rid of the fever, it was growing worse.

Then I was placed in front of the nurse's desk and a basin with clean water was placed on the stand beside me. I thought it was water placed there for me to drink. As I felt thirsty at the time, I used my hand and took three handfuls and swallowed.

And the nurse called to me and asked what did you do? Drink it?

I could not answer her. I really did not know what happened until I discovered about five doctors over me and found myself throwing up. And a few hours after I was settled, I noticed they drew some blood from my arm. I then noticed from that time there was no more of that bitter liquid. The whole night I was not bothered with that stuff.

The next morning, two men came with a stretcher and carried me off out of the ward. I thought they were going to bury me, as I was actually given over as dead.

However, I was taken to Ward 24, as it was called, the place where typhoid patients were being treated. They found out that the fever I had was typhoid and not malaria.

What I can truthfully say—those American nurses—my own dear mother could not be more kind and tender to me. I should right here tell of the incident with the water I drank from the basin on the stand beside my bed. It was poisoned water to kill flies that buzzed around.

George Hodges was employed in Culebra Cut as a powder man.

I can remember in the year 1913 we were notified by the boss to report to work Saturday morning early because we were going to have an important task to be carried out that day.

After we had all gathered together, Mr. Adams, who was my boss, called to me, "Hodges, come here." He asked me, "As you all the time have been going to the powder house, please let me know what kind of powder do you have up there?"

I, in turn, said to him that I have Keystone, Dupont, and Trojan.

He again asked me, "Hodges, what kind of powder do you think best to use to shoot those holes today?"

I immediately told him to take my advice and use the Trojan powder.

He said to me, "Why should you choose Trojan powder and leave out Keystone and Dupont—the best?"

I told him that I know that they are the best, but I prefer Trojan powder because you have a better chance with Trojan than the other two powders. In case of danger, Trojan powder will give you a sign.

He asked me, "What do you mean by a sign?"

I told him that the sign is that when the Trojan powder gets [hot in] the hole it boils like a pot and you can naturally hear it. But not Keystone and Dupont; whenever they get hot, they fire off right away.

Then one of the bosses, whose name was Jeffry, said to him, "He's right. Trojan powder is the best one to use today to do that job." And they all came to an agreement to use Trojan powder.

Then Jack took out his pocketbook and wrote to the watchman please to deliver to these men 175 boxes of dynamite. Each box contains 50 pounds [22.7 kg] . . . five packages, [each containing] twenty sticks.

Some of the holes were 30 feet [9.1 m] vertical, and some less. The toe holes were ten to 12 feet [3.7 m] deep. About five minutes after [John Sandyford and some men] started loading those holes, I heard Sandyford shout: "Look out, fellows!"

And when we did look, we saw the holes start to discharge one by one without any electrical wire attached to them. Then we realized what was going to happen and all the men had to run to save their lives.

So I was the man who advised the boss to use that Trojan powder, and if they had not heeded my advice, I would not be alive today to tell the story.

James A. Lewis described what could have happened.

My first and greatest experience was the steam shovel. The way the engineer worked that lever—you should see that long arm slide out and down, coming up with the bucket full of dirt and rocks and dumping it on the train with flat cars.

There were drilling gangs and powder gangs. The drilling gangs drill the holes in the earth with diamond or tripod drills. The powder gangs come and fill the holes with dynamite and ram it, and sometimes the hole gets hot and explodes.

I was brakeman when this happened. We were getting a load of dirt at the steam shovel and a powder gang was on the other side filling the holes with dynamite and ramming it. Well, we got our trainload of dirt and left the steam shovel. In fifteen minutes there was an explosion and that powder gang was blown up. On the track lines you could see parts of men's bodies. It's an awful sight to see.

For an interesting reason, George H. Martin remembered that his boss sent him to clean debris from the water that filled newly constructed locks. "We were to seize two stumps or bodies of trees that had floated on the water and nail them together like rafts. Two of us would have to get on this and go in the water and clean it of all the debris that had floated, for the water brought everything to the top, except stones. We had to bring all those things to shore, and that was how the locks were cleared of debris. The thing that had me so scared was that I could swim but like lead."

U.S. Post Office wagon at work in the Panama Canal Zone during early days of construction

Chapter 4

WHY THE CANAL SUCCEEDED

When the United States undertook to build a canal in Panama, President Theodore Roosevelt was well acquainted with the tragedy suffered by Jules Dingler and the other men and women who had tried to build a canal for France. Roosevelt gave public health first priority. Dr. William Crawford Gorgas was appointed to make the Canal Zone a healthy place. This proved to be one of the secrets for successfully building a canal at Panama.

Gorgas was an Army doctor with very special qualifications. He was immune to yellow fever because he had caught the disease while treating victims of an epidemic at Brownsville, Texas. When he recovered, he had lifetime immunity. Because of his immunity, he was posted to Havana, Cuba, during the Spanish-American War.

Havana was full of yellow fever, and Major Walter Reed's experiments confirmed that *Aëdes aegypti* mosquitoes [1] carry the virus and infect humans by biting them. Gorgas diligently destroyed every place where mosquitoes could breed in the entire city of Havana, thus eradicating both mosquitoes and yellow fever there.

In June 1904, Gorgas arrived in Panama to work his magic again. But for a year, managers failed to buy supplies he asked for and employees ignored his ideas and directions. Then John Frank Stevens arrived to take over as the new chief engineer. Stevens bought the materials and assigned men to work for Gorgas.

The Gorgas team went everywhere. They installed screens to prevent mosquitoes from entering buildings. They poured insecticides into holes

John Frank Stevens, the railroad man who designed the high-level lake canal and assembled the equipment and people to build it

and drainage ditches to kill mosquito larvae. Some men chased and captured individual mosquitoes that somehow got inside screened dormitories.

After six months, Gorgas had eliminated yellow fever from the Canal Zone. He also eliminated almost all malaria, which is carried by another type of mosquito, the *Anopheles*. Gorgas directed other work that made the Canal Zone a healthful place to live, but his victory over yellow fever made him a legend in his own time.

John Stevens is the second American worth special notice. He figured out how to actually build the canal. When Stevens arrived in Panama, he envisioned building a sea-level canal, a "wide expanse of blue, rippling water and great ships plowing their way through it, like the Straits of Magellan." Originally he thought a sea-level canal meant "only a little more depth to dig and a little more money."[2]

What changed his mind were the months of October and November. Those months, the stormiest each year, bring the Chagres River to flood stage. "The one great problem in the construction of any canal down there is the control of the Chagres River," Stevens told Congress. "That overshadows *everything* else.[3]

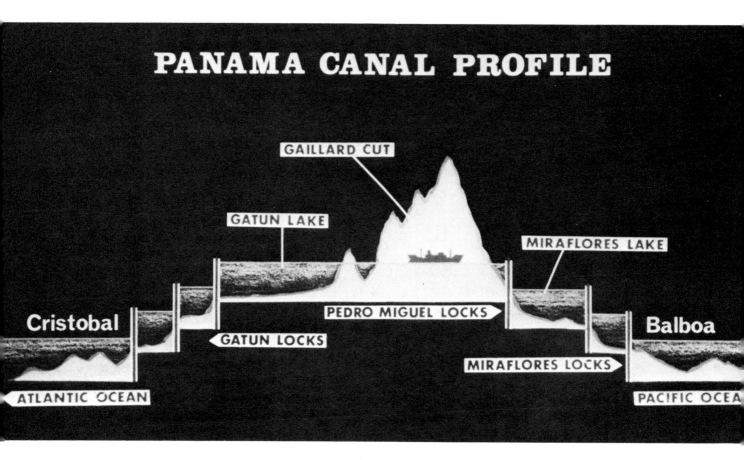

PANAMA CANAL PROFILE

GAILLARD CUT

GATUN LAKE

MIRAFLORES LAKE

Cristobal

PEDRO MIGUEL LOCKS

GATUN LOCKS

MIRAFLORES LOCKS

Balboa

ATLANTIC OCEAN

PACIFIC OCEA

Artist's profile of high-level lake design for the Panama Canal

What Stevens taught Congress was that any plan for a sea-level canal automatically created an enemy: the Chagres River. In dry months, the Chagres was quiet; in rainy months, it became powerful and terrifying. The river is fed by about 1,289 square miles (3,339 sq km) of watershed, steep slopes with rock so near the surface that the soil cannot absorb rain. Tropical storms can raise the Chagres to a violent flood stage in minutes.

The alternative to a sea-level canal was a high-level lake design. This approach would make the Chagres a friend instead of an enemy. Credit for first publicly suggesting a high-level lake canal belongs to Frenchman Adolphe Godin de Lepinay. In 1879, at France's Interoceanic Canal Congress, he recommended creating two lakes 80 feet (24.4 m) above sea level and connecting them with a cut dug through the continental divide at Culebra. His suggestion was not taken seriously.

In 1906, a few people suggested it again. The majority of a committee appointed by President Roosevelt recommended a sea-level canal forty feet deep and 150 feet wide, but a minority argued that the high-level lake design would be better.

The "Battle of the Levels" was debated in Congress in the spring of 1906. Even after Stevens and other witnesses testified, feelings in favor of a sea-level canal remained very strong. When the Senate voted on June 19, 1906, the vote was 36 to 31—if three senators had switched their votes, the sea-level design would have been attempted.

Choosing the high-level lake design proved to be another secret for successfully building a canal at Panama.

John Stevens created the organization and bought the equipment that was able to build the canal. He aimed to employ as few workers as possible. "[T]he introduction of every device that could do away with common labor was very imperative," he said. Hand labor was slow, and required hiring, housing, and feeding huge numbers of people, and therefore was too expensive to be practical. "[T]he canal would have cost fourfold what it did, and its time of completion no man could have safely predicted." [4]

Before Stevens came to Panama, he built railroads in the western United States. In Panama, Stevens built a system of tracks that kept empty rail cars at the steam shovels every moment so digging would never be delayed. He double-tracked the "transcontinental" Panama Railroad so trains could haul excess dirt unceasingly. And he hauled the dirt to the ends of the canal, Gatun and La Boca, to build dams and fill swamps.

The Stevens era became known as the railroad era. Everything important moved by rail. No cars, trucks, or bulldozers were used to build the canal. Stevens's railroad was another secret of building a canal successfully at Panama. The French had used trains, too, but only to haul dirt from excavations to nearby hills.

Stevens organized construction around four labor-saving devices. The first was the 95-ton (105 mt) Bucyrus steam shovel. Coal fed its fire, steam powered its mechanism, and seven to ten men operated it: an engineer on the controls, a craneman to dump dirt from the scoop, one fireman or two stokers to shovel coal, and a move-up crew of four to six men to lay railroad track in front of the shovel so it could roll forward to dig new ground.

With each swing of its bucket, the Bucyrus shoveled about 8 tons (8.8 mt) of rock and dirt. This "spoil" was dumped onto railroad cars and hauled away. The all-time shoveling record was set in March 1910 by

Major William Sibert, with umbrella, was in charge of building Gatun Locks and Gatun Dam. Before coming to Panama, he had built locks and dams on the Allegheny, Monongahela, and Ohio rivers in the United States.

Shovel 123. In twenty-six days, its crew excavated about 224 million pounds—almost a scoop every working minute.

The Bucyrus efficiency would have been wasted without a constant stream of railroad cars to haul the spoil away. With fifty to sixty-eight shovels working, it took 150 trainloads to haul the dirt away every day.

Stevens bought a mixture of self-dumping cars and flatcars. The flatcars proved most useful. Built wider than standard railroad cars, they could hold a large amount of spoil. Because they were flatcars, they could be quickly and completely unloaded in any weather, even when rock and mud clogged the self-dumping cars.

What unloaded the flatcars was labor saver number two: the Lidgerwood System, a plow that swept each flatcar clean.

The flatcars were built with one raised side against which spoil was banked. The space between cars was spanned by a steel plate, a bridge to carry the plow from one car to the next. At the spoils dump, the Lidgerwood plow would start on the last car of the train and be winched forward over all the cars, shoving spoil over the flatcar's low side onto the ground beside the tracks. The plow could clean a twenty-car train in ten minutes.

The third labor saver was the dirt spreader. Like a snowplow, it was pushed through the dumped spoil by a locomotive. When it had spread two or three loads of dirt over a wider area, the entire length of track was shifted sideways onto the new dirt so spoil would be dumped and spread in a new area.

The machine that shifted tracks was labor saver number four. William G. Bierd, manager of the Panama Railroad, invented it. He saw landslides bend steel railroad tracks like taffy, and that gave him the idea that steel tracks were flexible, not rigid. He invented the track shifter, a crane strong enough to lift a complete section of track, without disassembling rails from ties, and set it down 3 to 9 feet (.9 to 2.7 m) to one side.

To do this by hand, spikes had to be pulled, rails lifted, ties moved, rails relaid and gauged and respiked. By using the track shifter, said Stevens, "an ordinary train crew of five men and a locomotive, with half a dozen laborers, did the equivalent amount of work that before its introduction required about two hundred laborers, and in much less time."[5]

The day Bierd's invention was first tested, it moved more than 1 mile (1.6 km) of track in just ten hours.

In January 1907, Stevens wrote President Roosevelt that he no longer was happy in his job. Roosevelt accepted that as Stevens's resignation and chose a successor.

Labor saver #1:
The 95-ton Bucyrus
steam shovel could
lift eight tons of rock
in its scoop.

Labor saver #2:
The Lidgerwood System
plow could sweep clean
a twenty-car dirt
train in ten minutes.

Labor saver #3:
The dirt spreader was
pushed through soil dumped
by the Lidgerwood plow to
spread it over a wider area.

Labor saver #4:
William G. Bierd invented
the track shifter after
he saw landslides bend
steel railroad tracks like
taffy, teaching him tracks
were flexible, not rigid.

"I was summoned to the White House by President Roosevelt," recalled Major George Washington Goethals, U.S. Army. "He said that it was impossible to think of a successful prosecution of the work with frequent changes of leadership, since an efficient and permanent force could not be maintained under such conditions, and that he had decided to place it in the charge of men who could not resign unless he desired them to do so—to place the task in the hands of Army engineers, thereby securing continuity of service." [6]

Roosevelt made another decision at the same time. Congress had ordered that a committee oversee the work. Roosevelt said the committee created trouble and friction. To solve the problem, he appointed a new committee, named Goethals the chairman, and told every other member that Goethals "is to have complete authority. If at any time you do not agree with his policies, do not bother to tell me about it—your disagreement with him will constitute your resignation." [7]

That made George W. Goethals absolute ruler of the Canal Zone. Journalist Arthur Bullard observed Goethals's power firsthand. He was allowed to sit in Goethals's office one Sunday, the day Goethals always made himself available to hear workers' complaints.

The first callers were a . . . couple from Jamaica. They had a difference of opinion as to the ownership of 35 dollars which the wife had earned by washing. Colonel Goethals listened gravely until the fact was established that she had earned it, then ordered the man to return it. He started to protest something about a husband's property rights under the English law. "All right," the Colonel said, decisively. "Say the word, and I'll deport you. You can get all the English law you want in Jamaica." The husband decided to pay and stay. . . .

An American . . . was convinced that his services were of more value than his foreman felt they were. The Colonel preferred to accept the foreman's judgment in the matter. The dissatisfied one pompously announced that he was the best blacksmith's helper on the Isthmus and he intended to appeal from this decision. The Colonel's eyes twinkled. "To whom are you going to appeal?" he asked. "For the fact is that the verdicts rendered in these summary Sunday sessions will not be revised before the Day of Judgment." [8]

The secret Goethals brought to the canal was persistence. He won fame for being everywhere for seven years. Famous landslides occurred in Culebra Cut during the Goethals era. Many people had ideas for easy ways

George Goethals, umbrella in hand, on foot to inspect
the Miraflores Locks and dam creating Miraflores Lake

In 1913, a landslide at Culebra Cut spilled rock into the still-dry canal channel and required more than eighteen months to completely clear away. Dredges finished the job after water filled the channel.

Track gang at work on bent rails after landslide in Culebra Cut

to stop the slides—people who knew little about geology and who had never been to Panama. Goethals coped by persistence: he kept digging.

Geologists discovered that hilltops along the Cut often were hard, heavy rock shaped like ice-cream cones, large and heavy at the top and narrow at the bottom. The "ice cream" dome was the visible hilltop, and the "cone" was buried in a sea of weaker rock. As digging deepened the Cut, the new rock walls proved too weak to support the heavy hilltops above them and were squeezed into the Cut.

The logical solution was to remove the weight. Goethals had the hilltops dug away. Originally the Cut was to be a narrow gorge with steep banks. Now the hilltops are cut so far back that most banks of the Cut are gentle slopes. More than twice the rock was excavated than was planned. Twice the rock meant at least twice the work.

In 1913, another landslide—the largest yet—occurred at a spot in the Cut known as Cucaracha—Cockroach. Colonel David D. Gaillard, supervisor of work in the Cut, felt discouraged and said to Goethals, "What are we ever going to do now?"

"H——!" replied Goethals. "Dig it out again."[9]

Electricians, around 1913, with brand-new transformers and electrical switches installed by the General Electric Company to power the canal

Chapter 5

A NATION DIVIDED

The president of Panama, Belisario Porras, rode aboard a small ship, the *Ancon,* when it made the inaugural transit of the new Panama Canal on August 15, 1914.

George Goethals, America's senior official at the canal, was not aboard the *Ancon* that day. It may have been Goethals's intent to give Porras a starring role. We can only guess, but there is reliable evidence that Goethals had shown sensitivity to Panamanian feelings and pride at least once before.

C. M. Saville, resident engineer in charge of meteorology, hydrography and land surveys, compiled a new map of the Canal Zone and adjacent areas. Some of the larger hills were given names of Americans connected with the Canal work and such new geographical designations as "Mount Goethals," "Mount Priscilla," and "Rousseau River" appeared on the draft of the new map.

When the map was submitted to Colonel Goethals, his eyes fell upon these names. "Haven't these places already got native names?" he inquired.

"Yes, sir," was the reply, "but—"

Colonel Goethals raised his hand. Picking up his well-known indelible pencil, he drew lines through a few of the newly provided American names which had been meant to honor the first families of the Canal regime. "I think the native names will do very well," he said.[1]

George Goethals
watches the *Ancon*
enter the locks of
the Panama Canal on
opening day in 1914.

During the "first transit," Goethals spent all day ashore watching the *Ancon*'s progress. He was worried. Problems had developed during practice transits.

On August 3, when the *Cristobal* entered Gatun Locks, it encountered strong currents that nearly slammed the ship into the lock walls. It was in a precarious position, but was brought under control by the towing locomotives, one of which burned out an electric motor and was disabled.

Later, at Pedro Miguel Locks, a towing locomotive broke the steel cable it was using to control the *Cristobal*. "When the vessel was brought into the locks, things looked rather squally, and I feared damage to the gates, but they succeeded in stopping her in time. At the upper lock at Miraflores a similar condition [existed], but I telephoned down and they were using three locomotives on either side and the ship was halted much more easily."[2]

The August 3 troubles surprised Goethals. "The . . . affairs which arose made it impossible for me to accept the responsibility of an accident, due to the landlubbers in charge of the ship . . . "[3] He gave the Navy charge of the ships and towing locomotives.

The change delighted Navy Captain Hugh Rodman. Goethals originally wanted ships to stop at lock entrances, take canal employees on board, and fasten cables from towing locomotives. Rodman, a seafarer, wanted the ships to already have pilots aboard, keep moving, and fasten cables while still under way.

For the *Ancon*'s inaugural transit, they did it Rodman's way. Goethals still was worried and watchful. But practice had made perfect. The *Ancon*'s transit was peaceful, under complete control. A guest on board later congratulated Goethals on the ease with which the canal operated, "as if the Canal had been completed and in operation for many years."[4]

The *Ancon* entered the Atlantic entrance to the canal shortly after 7 A.M. and sailed into the Pacific Ocean nine hours and forty minutes later. When it docked at the canal's Pacific end, two thousand people were on hand to cheer.

What a triumph for the engineers! They had built a staircase to carry ocean liners over the mountains from sea to sea. At each set of locks, one person with a twist of a wrist could start or stop the flow of the 26 million gallons (98.4 million l) of water that fill a lock chamber or open or close lock gates that weighed up to 770 tons (848.5 mt).

And the engineers had built this canal to operate without one single pump. All of the tons of water that lifted and lowered ships simply flowed with gravity.

Americans who built the canal considered it one of their nation's greatest engineering achievements. And Panamanians began to consider the Panama Canal their nation's greatest natural resource.

Natural resource? The Panama Canal is entirely manmade, but confusion arises because forty-seven of its fifty miles are formed from nature's elements: earth, rock, and water.

Photograph taken by U.S. weather satellite shows how the Panama
Canal physically divides the Republic of Panama.

Not long after the water was let into Culebra Cut and the Gamboa Dike had been blown up and dredged away, the U.S. Secretary of War paid a visit of inspection to the Canal. Colonel Goethals took him out to Gamboa, where they boarded a tugboat for a trip through the northern part of the Cut to the slides at Culebra and Cucaracha.

Between Bas Obispo and Las Cascadas, the Cut had been completed for some time and . . . tropical vegetation had already covered the scars of excavation. The men were silent, listening to the steady rhythm of the tugboat's engines and the quiet sweep of water off the bow.

The secretary remarked very solemnly, "It seems like God Almighty must have meant for us to build a canal here, seeing"—indicating with a wave of his hand—"how He provided this natural channel for our use."

The colonel explained that the channel had been a mountain blasted and dug from a height of 100 feet (30.5 m) above them to a depth of 40 feet (12.2 m) below, and pointed out the spot nearby where a premature explosion of dynamite in 1908 had killed twenty-six of the canal workers.[5]

Panama's citizens, from the start, expected the canal to put money into their pockets. Some money did flow to them, but they expected and wanted more. The major problem was a psychological one. Panamanians did not feel they were part of the Panama Canal operation. They felt Americans excluded them from this "grand undertaking." They felt discriminated against.

And because this canal cut through the heart of their nation, they felt it was terribly wrong for Panamanians to be treated as outsiders.

Some complaints were very specific. As early as May 1904, when the United States published regulations for administering the new Canal Zone, Panamanians complained that no one had shown the regulations to them.

They complained that the United States defined exactly where Canal Zone boundaries would be—without consulting Panama. They complained that the United States imported large numbers of laborers to build the canal, mostly from British islands in the Caribbean. It was true. Canal managers wanted workers who spoke English. They said Spanish-speaking native Panamanians accomplished less work in a day. Panamanians were not hired to build the Panama Canal.

The United States built restaurants and stores that sold merchandise in the Canal Zone at New Orleans prices so canal employees could avoid shopping in Panamanian stores that were "too small," "too poorly stocked," or "too expensive." Canal stores also sold goods to transiting ships: fuel, food, laundry service (dirty clothes were collected as the ship entered the canal and were delivered cleaned as it exited to sea), and ship repairs. Panamanians complained these businesses robbed them of money they had expected to earn.

Panamanians calculated thousands of dollars ships paid in tolls. The annual rent they received from the United States seemed far too small a share of the proceeds being earned by . . . well, by *Panama's* canal!

The United States took control of a quarry to get rock needed to build the locks at Gatun. It took sand from Punta de Chame beach. It built military facilities at several locations in Panama. Panamanians complained that they had lost control of their own national territory, that the United States went anywhere it pleased and took any land it wanted.

Street in the village of Cruces in 1912. The construction of Gatun Lake buried villages like this underwater.

Ships of all nations were required by the United States, operator of the canal, to fly the Stars and Stripes while in transit. Panamanians wanted ships to fly the flag of Panama, the sovereign and host nation.

Americans, on the other hand, wanted no one to forget that the United States had paid hard cash for the canal four times! Ten million dollars to Panama, plus rent each year. Forty million dollars to France to buy out French rights to a canal in Panama. Twenty-five million dollars to Colombia because that nation claimed ownership of the land before Panama seceded. And more than $300 million to actually dig the ditch, erect the locks, flood the canal with water, and start the first ship on its way through.

The canal was not a financial success in American eyes, either. During construction days, U.S. government money paid for everything from 1904 to 1914. When the canal opened in 1914, shipowners began sharing the costs. Tolls were charged "to offset, at least in part, the cost of the maintenance and operation of the canal and the interest on the money invested in it."[6]

Rules for charging tolls were so confused during the canal's first twenty-three years of operation that two sister ships of exactly the same size and cargo capacity were charged different tolls. The *Gold Shell* and the *Silver Shell* had one difference: a fuel transfer pump installed in a different location. One paid $4,386 each transit and the other $5,076.

Some ships paid as much—or as little—when empty as when full. Tugboats sometimes transited at no charge because the rules measured them at zero tons—or less than zero!

Congress adjusted the rules in 1938, but still kept tolls low and continued to subsidize canal operations. Not until 1951 did Congress direct the canal to charge shipowners enough to pay all costs.

"To Americans unacquainted with the peculiar conditions on the Isthmus," said canal governor Jay J. Morrow in 1923, "this intrusion of their Government into industries which are commonly conducted by private enterprise may cause surprise."[7] Panama seemed too small, too poorly developed, and lacking in businesses properly able to support the large canal organization and all transiting ships.

"It is possible," Governor Morrow said, "that with the development of trade at Panama there will come a day when the [canal] business is large enough to justify participation by one or more well-equipped companies, and when this time comes it will be found that the Government will gladly yield to private industry such parts of the work as can be effectively handled by ordinary business methods."

Americans proudly displayed the American flag in the Canal Zone.
Here George Goethals speaks at a Fourth of July celebration.

Bridge of the Americas, at the canal's Pacific end, is the first
full-time link established across the canal between east and west
Panama. It is purposely high at the center to prevent interference
with any ship transiting the canal.

Americans pointed to very real benefits Panama was reaping. The country wasn't all swamp and jungle, malaria and yellow fever anymore. Americans had made Panama City and Colón healthy. They had paved streets, installed clean running water and sewers, provided electricity, and improved schools.

And Americans waved the 1903 treaty, which said the United States could act like a sovereign in the Canal Zone forever.

The canal divided Panama both geographically and psychologically. A road to political success in Panama developed: voice anti-Yankee feelings. Polarization made the gap even wider. In politics, polarization forces people to take sides, to be counted against something if they are not entirely for it, or to be counted for something if not entirely against it. Polarization ignores in-betweens. It is often felt that there could not be any middle ground, that no intelligent person could hold a moderate, compromising view.

In Panama, politicians were not allowed to be nationalist (pro-Panama) *and* pro-American. They were forced to be nationalist *or* pro-American. This psychology remains effective today.

While the Panama Canal is a bridge of water connecting two oceans, building it ripped Panama asunder. The nation has not yet recovered from the turmoil.

Not until 1962 was there a permanent, full-time bridge to join the east and west banks of the canal. In that year, a steel highway bridge opened at the canal's Pacific end. Ricardo Alfaro, former president of Panama and justice at the International Court of Justice in The Hague, called it a "colossal bridge that will re-establish continuity in the land divided by the Panama Canal . . ."[8]

Chapter 6

SPECIAL
PEOPLE

Panamanians felt unhappy and polarized because the canal divided their nation. They felt like outsiders because they were not hired to be canal employees. In contrast, Americans and people of any nationality who did win canal jobs developed exceptional pride and high morale.

Panama Canal training handbooks say no port anywhere in the world guarantees the safety of a ship in its waters to the same degree as the Panama Canal. Such safety for large ships in narrow waters depends on superb ability, judgment, and seamanship on the part of canal pilots and a host of other employees. Emergencies occasionally test employees' skills, courage, and intelligence. They respond well.

One example of a special skilled person working at the canal is Shep Shreaves. The United States awarded a Silver Lifesaving Medal to Shep ''for heroic efforts in rescuing two men from a sunken U.S. submarine, October 29, 1923.''

It all started when Captain W. A. Card of the SS *Abangarez* ''[h]ove up our anchor at 6:14 A.M. and proceeded towards Pier 8 at various speeds.'' The *Abangarez* was crossing Limon Bay, the Atlantic entrance to the Panama Canal.

When nearly abreast of No. 4 channel buoy [I] saw submarine 0-5 apparently stopped off the Mole Buoy and taking on Pilot. At this time she was on the Abangarez' *Port bow and started to move ahead slowly as if to clear stern of SS* Arawa *backing out from Pier 6. When the submarine was clear of the SS* Arawa *I noticed an increase in her speed as if trying*

SS *Abangarez*

U.S. Navy submarine *O-5*

*to cross our bow. As soon as I decided that was [her] intention I blew
the danger signal, put our engines at full speed astern and let go our
starboard anchor with fifteen fathoms of chain.*

*At 6:24 A.M. we struck the submarine at right angles amidships on
her Starboard side causing her to sink in a few minutes.*[1]

Rescuers pulled sixteen sailors from the water; five were still missing.

A Navy salvage tug rushed divers to the collision site. Quickly they
located the *o-5* on the harbor floor, rapped on the sub's hull, and seemed
to hear raps from inside. Someone was trapped alive!

The Panama Canal owned the two largest floating cranes in the world,
each able to lift 250 tons (275.5 mt). One, the U.S. *Ajax,* began sailing
to the rescue. A landslide at Culebra Cut blocked the way, but two dipper
dredges cleared a path for *Ajax* to slip through. By 10:30 P.M., *Ajax* was
over the wreck.

Shep Shreaves volunteered to dive. He was supervisor of the canal's
salvage and diving crew.

Shep donned a deep-sea diving suit and found the *o-5* by following
a chain of air bubbles. "I went right in through the hole in her side. The
light of my lamp was feeble against the black pitch. Inside it was an
awful mess. It was tight and slippery. I was constantly pushing away
floating debris."

Shep was in danger. Jagged metal could cut the hose that brought
him fresh air from the surface, or debris could foul his hose, trapping
him in the sub.

*When I reached the forward bulkhead of the engine room I rapped with
my diving hammer. Faint taps were returned. Someone was still alive. I
acknowledged with a feeling of hopelessness, as I could do no more at
the time.*

*I emerged from the o-5. By prearrangement I signaled to lower the
fire hose. The o-5 lay upright in several feet of soft mud. I began jetting
a trench under her bow. Sluicing through the muck was easy—too easy,
for it could cave in on me. Swirling black engulfed me, and I worked by
feel and instinct. I had to be careful not to dredge too much from under
the bow, for the o-5 could crush down on me. Occasionally I'd hit the
hull to let the boys inside know someone was working to save them. Weak
taps were returned each time.*[2]

Shep succeeded in jetting a narrow trench and pulled a thin guideline
through it. Men on the surface used the guideline to drag a strong, four-

Shep Shreaves

inch-diameter steel cable under the submarine. Both ends were fastened to *Ajax*'s lifting hook. *Ajax* lifted. The cable broke.

A local newspaper, the *Star & Herald*, reported:

Up to midnight efforts to raise the sunken sub had failed and it was feared the imprisoned members of the crew would perish before the craft could be raised. Divers who have rapped against the outside of the sunken submarine have received replies from within, but the imprisoned sailors do not know the Morse code and are unable to give any information as to how many are imprisoned. Their responses to the dots and dashes rapped out on the outside of the sunken craft have been a series of un-intelligible knocks.[3]

For a second time, Shep snaked a guideline through the trench. Another four-inch cable was pulled through. *Ajax* lifted. The cable broke again.

Shep went under the submarine a third time. The cable broke a third time.

Shep had been diving for almost twenty-four hours. Navy doctors worried that he would collapse from exhaustion or that his heart would fail under the strain.

Shep tried once more. Two things held the submarine down: one was simply the weight of the flooded craft; the other, the suction of bottom mud wrapped around the hull. To reduce the sub's weight, Shep aimed a jet of compressed air into the engine room. As water and mud boiled to the surface, *Ajax* began to pull gently for the fourth time.

Shep sensed the moment was right. He signaled *Ajax* to begin lifting in earnest. The bow of the *0-5* began to rise. From 12:30 to 1:10 P.M., *Ajax* pulled. Then the sub's bow broke surface.

Two survivors crawled out after thirty-one hours of imprisonment: Chief Electrician's Mate Lawrence Brown and Torpedoman Second Class Henry Breault.

Shep Shreaves demonstrated exceptional skill and courage. Panama Canal employees have pointed with pride to similar excellence among many fellow workers. Foremost recognition has been given to the pilots who board ships, take command, and move them safely through the canal.

"Used to be," a pilot said, "a person who wanted to be a pilot had to have been master of [an oceangoing] vessel for at least a year and be under 35 years of age. That meant a young captain—the canal got top performers."

Required qualifications changed in recent years. The canal began to accept experience as a second or third officer of a merchant ship or experience as a tugboat captain for five years. Age rules were waived.

Pilot Rodney Robertson, worried about the changes in qualifications and requirements, in 1974 wrote a dramatic, fictionalized article to urge a return to the old requirements.

The Holocaust at Coal Hoist Bend
by R. R. Robertson

It's a hot, muggy afternoon in the summer of 1980 and traffic is moving in the busy Panama Canal. The passenger vessel Andros Castle *has cleared Pedro Miguel Locks northbound and is making her course change to starboard around Gold Hill into Culebra Reach. Her 2,100 passengers who had been on deck enjoying the view through the locks have now taken shelter below decks as a steady rain begins to fall. On the bridge in charge of the vessel's navigation is a Panama Canal pilot who everyone calls "captain," unaware that he holds no recognized maritime certificate.*

Southbound, approaching La Pita signal station, is the deeply laden motor tanker Ta Cheng, *carrying 30,000 tons [33,060 t] of gasoline cargo.*

[62]

Canal-launch captain reaches out to help *O-5* survivor Henry Breault
aboard after the *Ajax* finally pulled the submarine to the surface.

On the bridge in control of the navigation is another Panama Canal pilot who, like his colleague on the Andros Castle, *had never set foot on the bridge of an ocean-going vessel until he was hired as a pilot-in-training by the Panama Canal Company. As the* Ta Cheng *swings slowly to port into Empire Reach, the rains increase to a blinding torrent in the truest tradition of the Panama rainy season. The visibility is suddenly reduced to the point that sailing ranges and other navigational aids are no longer visible to the pilots on either vessel. The pilot on the* Ta Cheng *orders the helmsman to steady on a compass course but, since the gyro compass is inoperative, there is only a magnetic compass to steer by. The pilot, unschooled in the matters of magnetism and compass correction, makes the deadly error of applying his course correction in the opposite direction than that called for, causing his vessel to close steadily with the rocky banks of Coal Hoist Bend. Although both vessels are equipped with radar, it is of little value in this torrential rain. Besides, neither pilot has any experience in its use nor ever been certified as a qualified radar observer.*

Suddenly, the horror-stricken pilot on the Ta Cheng *sees the bank close on the starboard bow and puts his helm hard to port and engines full ahead in a vain effort to avoid striking the bank. In his short maritime career this pilot had never had occasion to use an anchor for turning or stopping a ship and, of course, according to operating procedures, this vessel no longer rated a tug on the stern to assist him in this perilous situation.*

The Ta Cheng *careened off the west bank, slicing open four cargo tanks as she did so, and with speed built up by the emergency maneuvers, shot across the channel toward the east bank and rammed her bow deep into the port midships section of the* Andros Castle. *With the channel rapidly filling with gasoline, unchecked fires starting from the heat generated by the collision, and with both vessels locked together as they settle slowly to the bottom, only the calmest decisions by an experienced shipmaster could minimize loss of life and property damage.*

But consider this: Neither pilot had ever seen, let alone supervised, a fire and boat drill. Nor did they have the slightest idea of the principles of damage control, vessel stability, or how to curb the inevitable panic such a situation creates.

And when the stunned world recovers from the shock of the loss of over 2,000 lives in the holocaust at Coal Hoist Bend, the inevitable questions will be asked: Why? Who is to blame? Don't look to the hapless pilots who were given jobs they were not properly qualified to perform.[4]

The specific accident Rod Robertson foresaw hasn't happened yet. It is hoped that it never will.

Canal pilots have an awesome responsibility. There can be terrible consequences from any ship accident. The accident canal pilots fear most is collision with a ship carrying dangerous cargo. "It could happen in the channel off Balboa . . . near the bridge," says pilot Tim Kirkby. "My house is [near there], within the area that would be damaged by such an explosion. I worry about that."

A canal pilot's normal day often starts with a 4 A.M. wakeup call from the canal dispatcher. The pilot packs his "office" in a soft leather bag that's easy to haul aboard ship: walkie-talkies, extra batteries, reference books, and a change of clothes. Within the hour, he rides a launch into the Pacific anchorage to board "his" ship. It's an hour before sunrise, the hour of "first light."

Today's ship, called "North Six," is the NS-*Alliance*. It's about 800 feet (244 m) long. This pilot's assignment is "first-half control pilot."

He aims North Six into the canal entrance. To a landlubber, it looks like water a mile wide, but the pilot knows banks hidden below water mark a much narrower channel. As North Six passes Balboa, the Pacific port, a launch leaves Pier 18, matches speed alongside, and three more pilots climb aboard. A second launch brings twenty canal deckhands to handle ropes and cables during transit of the first two locks.

North Six rounds a curve. The first locks, Miraflores, come into sight but North Four and Five are in the locks, so the pilot orders North Six's engines to slow.

It's 7 A.M. Time for breakfast. The first-half control pilot stays on post and is served on the bridge. The other three pilots go down two decks to the "saloon" for poached eggs on toast with ham.

By 7:30, pilots are posted at each side of the bow and each side of the bridge. North Six approaches the east lane of the locks. On order from the control pilot, three towing locomotives on the center wall hook steel cables to North Six. To starboard, a tug shoves the *Alliance*'s bow, trying to hold it within 2 feet (.6 m) of the wall.

As the ship glides forward, water flowing between hull and wall creates pressure that pushes the ship away. Because the ship is 106 feet (32.3 m) wide and the locks only 110 (33.5 m), the ship can't squeeze into the chamber unless the tug shoves it close to the center wall.

North Six enters the chamber at 3 miles an hour (5 kmh). Deckhands bring aboard cables from three more towing locomotives on the side wall. The four pilots watch their corners of the ship for any sign of drifting.

Ship enters a lock. Control pilot on bridge near ship's stern
depends on pilots at bow to watch their "corners" of the ship.

"Eighteen inches [457 mm] and closing," one reports by walkie-talkie.

"Side One," radios the control pilot. "Slack!" The front towing locomotive on the side wall slacks its cables, giving pull from locomotives on the center wall greater effect. The drift stops. The 2-foot (.6 m) clearance is reestablished.

"Side One. Resume towing." The cables tighten.

The tug floats into the chamber behind North Six. Behind it shut the miter gates, a pair of metal doors that seal the entrance so the chamber will hold water. Each gate has leaves 65 feet 7 inches (21 m) wide and 7 feet (2.13 m) thick. The leaves swing from hinges on each wall and meet at center chamberlike double doors. Since the leaves' combined width of 131 feet 2 inches (40 m) is greater than the 110-foot (33.5 m) lock width, they meet at an angle that always points toward high water, toward Lake Gatun. In operation, the pressure of high water forces the miter gates tightly shut. Indeed, until water levels on both sides of a gate are equal, it is "impossible" to open the leaves against the water pressure.

The locks have a total of 44 pairs of miter gates. Depending on where the gates are located, they range in height from 47 feet 4 inches (14.43 m) to 82 feet (25 m) and in weight from 440 to 770 tons (485 to 848.5 mt). They are watertight, buoyant like a ship's hull, so they can be opened or closed by a 25-horsepower (18.65 kw) motor or even, in an emergency, by handcranking the gears.

After the gates are closed, water flows into the chamber through 105 holes in the chamber floor.[5]

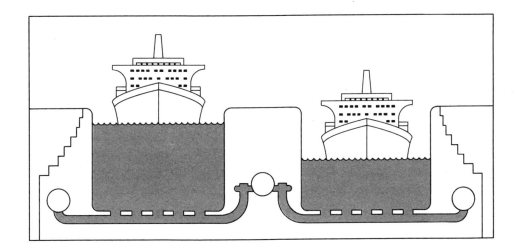

In 1928, travel writer Richard Halliburton swam through the canal and reported what he felt in the chamber. "The inflow is very violent and caused such whirlpools and suctions that I was forced to hold on to the [rowboat] *Daisy* as the submarine geysers boiled up and lifted, lifted me."[6]

After eight minutes, the chamber is filled, the ship has been lifted about 30 feet (9.1 m), the miter gates open, and towing locomotives guide North Six into the second chamber. To help, the control pilot orders ship's engines to half speed. Turbulent water from the prop rolls around the tug, making it bob roughly.

In the west lane, North Five is still locking upward. It's a tanker, a Panamax ship—the largest that can possibly squeeze into a chamber. Full of crude oil from Alaska, North Five is heavy, hard to move. Smaller and lighter, the *Alliance* steams out of its chamber first, crosses little Miraflores Lake—just a mile (1.6 km) long—and enters Pedro Miguel Locks.

The pilots watch every ship in sight, especially North Eight, trailing behind the *Alliance*. "The clumsiest ship that ever transited the canal," asserts one. The ship, remodeled to haul automobiles, has very high sides that catch the wind like uncontrollable sails.

"Look at him come! He's way too early. He has to wait another half hour before he can enter the [Miraflores] locks." North Eight continues toward the lock entrance. "He needs a tug bad. He's going to have to get a tug soon."

No tug is available. North Seven has two tugs; its pilot won't let either tug go. Risk *his* ship's safety? If North Eight's pilot is in trouble, it's his own fault and his own problem.

North Eight noses up to the Miraflores center wall. A single rope comes off the bow and the ship ties up. Currents catch the stern, pulling it away from the wall. The ship turns sideways in the channel.

On the pilots' walkie-talkie, the Miraflores lockmaster asks if North Eight is ready for the lock gates to be opened. "Not yet," answers North Eight's pilot. "Let's take our time." He needs a tug first.

Pedro Miguel's one lock lifts the *Alliance* the final 28-foot (8.5 m) step to Gatun Lake, the summit of the canal. The single tug lashes onto the stern to give extra power and control through the Cut.

The bow pilots leave their stations to nap in air-conditioned rooms. A launch matches speed, snugs its bow against the ship's ladder, and the deckhands debark.

After an hour, North Six releases its tug as it enters broad Gatun Lake. The second-half control pilot takes firm stance on the bridge, legs straddling the ship's centerline, and calls out, "I'll take it now."

Welcome words. The first-half control pilot disappears to find a room, a bed, and a two-hour nap. He has been on duty six hours, and the transit is barely half over.

Crossing Gatun Lake takes several hours. It covers an area of 163.38 square miles (423.1 square km), and when it was built it was the largest man-made lake in the world. "I remember being out here with a motorboat," says the second-half control pilot. "I was towing a water skier and I saw about a 12-foot [3.7 m] log floating in the water ahead, so I turned the boat to go around it. As we went by, I saw what the log really was: a crocodile."

He laughs. The captain of the *Alliance* laughs . . . then offers to buy crocodile hides.

"Not so many crocodile and alligators out here anymore," the pilot says. "Used to see a lot of them." North Six steams on, all eyes looking for gators.

At 11:45, North Six is still at full speed on Gatun Lake. The control pilot lunches on the bridge while the other three pilots sit in the saloon. The meal is steak. "You eat well on a Japanese ship," one pilot comments. "But the steak always is rare," mutters another. "I don't mind. It's always good." They recall delicious cheeses on Dutch ships, beer on others, and decide all canal pilots have "an international stomach."

The average ship waits eleven or twelve hours to begin transit, then spends approximately eight or nine hours sailing through. In 1979, one pilot aboard the *Alliance* today, John McKeen, took the U.S. Navy hydrofoil *Pegasus* through in two hours and 41 minutes—a new speed record.

About 1 P.M. North Six approaches Gatun Locks. A fresh tug ties on to push the starboard bow. "Where's our second tug?" The control pilot radios for it to "get a move on." Deckhands board. The *Alliance* collects six locomotives. Pilots cover their corners. In the west lane, a cruise ship is being lifted from the Atlantic to Gatun Lake.

In contrast to boiling waters that lifted North Six during up-lockage, descent is smooth. Water drains from the chamber with hardly a ripple. At the end of the three locks, the *Alliance* steams into the sea-level channel that leads to the Atlantic. A launch takes off deckhands, and soon another takes off the four pilots. The pilots will ride home by chauffered

Water "boils" into chamber through 110 holes in the chamber floor.

Locks are controlled by two operators using a panel built like a map of the locks, with switches, gauges, and model gates. Located on the top floor of the control house built on the lock's center wall, the panel operates a mechanical analog computer on the floor below.

sedan—"It's in our union contract!"—over the Trans-Isthmian Highway. It's an hour's drive, so this workday will end about 5 P.M.

"Fast transit," one pilot remarks. "If we'd had that tanker, North Five, we'd be two or three hours longer."

"At least two or three. He had to wait for eight cars [towing locomotives at Gatun Locks]."

Going home every night is a reward for Panama Canal pilots. Qualified ship captains normally are at sea for months at a time. Paychecks are a second reward. Pilots are experts; their pay is good. A third reward is watching the *Alliance* disappear over the horizon. They put that ship through the canal, ocean to ocean, in eight hours.

That's the mission of these special people.

Chapter 7

THE CHALLENGE

The challenge of yesteryear was answered by outstanding engineering used to build a canal that could join the oceans.

The challenge of today is being answered by good business practices that make the canal earn enough money to stay open.

When the canal first opened, advertising emphasized the miles and days a ship could save by using the canal instead of sailing around Cape Horn. The *Arizonan* was cited as an example.

"On the basis of a speed of 12 knots, the canal saves the *Arizonan* about 26.8 days at sea on each voyage from coast to coast."

The cost of operating the ship, $450 per day, meant the extra cost to sail around the Horn was about $11,700. Since the *Arizonan* paid a toll of only $7,891.20, the ship saved about $3,808 per voyage.[1]

When the canal first opened, most passengers and cargo were bound from one coast of the United States to the other. Today, few ships sail coast to coast. This route has slipped to eighth place. Trucks, planes, trains, and pipelines handle much of that business now.

Moreover, superships too large to fit through the Panama Canal haul other cargo, and two competitors carry shipments from one ocean to the other: pipelines for fluids like petroleum, and "overland bridges" composed of truck and railroad shipments.

SRI International, a renowned "think tank," studied the canal for Congress in 1967 because Congress wanted to know whether it could charge more for passage through the canal.

Aboard a ship, containers can be stacked like blocks. A tug
holds this ship along the center wall at Pedro Miguel Locks.

Bright, high mast lights opened Miraflores Locks
to large ships at night.

The "proper question," SRI pointed out, is what choices do ship owners have? Can they avoid paying higher tolls?

Indeed, ship owners have so many other alternatives that charging higher tolls could drive them away and reduce total money earned by the canal. Some people considered that a "somewhat surprising finding."[2]

Four other options open to ship owners are to change routes, use bigger ships, change ports of call, or change their entire pattern of business.

To change ship routes can be easy. About a million tons (1.102 million t) of sugar rides ships from the Philippines each year. The ships that now sail east to use the Panama Canal could sail west, use the Suez Canal, and reach the same ports. It's only 100 miles (161 km) farther.

Larger ships, superships, are already in use for petroleum and coal. They are too wide, too long, and too deep to fit into the locks. They also are so cheap to operate that their owners wouldn't use the canal if they could. For a tanker drawing 84 feet (25.6 m) of water, if somehow it could be squeezed into the canal, the toll would be more than $278,000. Sailing a few extra days on a longer route costs much less.

In fact, superships carry coal from the United States to Japan by sailing around Africa's Cape of Good Hope. It's thirteen extra days, but one-third cheaper.

To change ports of call, a ship owner uses trucks, trains, or pipelines to carry cargo part of the way. Goods going to Japan can be trucked to ports on the United States west coast, avoiding transit of the canal.

"Land bridge" and "minibridge" are two names given to the concept of shipping by sea plus road, rail, or pipeline. Truck-size containers and dockside cranes to lift them are the technological improvements that made the bridge possible.

The ship owners' fourth choice, changing the pattern of business, can be simple or complicated. A simple change would be to sell Chile's iron ore to Japan instead of to Europe so it could be shipped without using the canal. A complicated change would be to dig new mines in Asia or Africa instead of Chile.

In October 1982, Panama opened a pipeline across the isthmus, allowing tankers to pump oil from a ship in the Pacific to a ship in the Atlantic without transiting the canal. To compensate for that "bridge," canal managers raised tolls. Even that failed to prevent a financial crisis. Six fewer ships used the canal each day, and the canal spent four million dollars more than it earned that year.

Since then, there have been three trends. First, the number of transits each year has remained fairly steady at about 13,000. Second, the ships using the canal tend to be larger every year. Third, total income from tolls has increased each year.

Yet despite the increase in income, the canal since 1980 has made a profit only two years out of every three. The canal lost money in 1981, 1983, and 1987. On the average, it earns a profit of about one million dollars a year. That's less than .5 percent.

More than 60 percent of all tolls are paid by only 20 percent of the ships, the biggest ships. But little ships require as much work to transit as big ones do. The United States deliberately chose not to penalize small ships. All ships are handled on a first-come, first-served basis, with tolls computed the same way for every customer. (Exceptions are warships and passenger ships, which are entitled to priority passage. Yachts recently have been allowed to transit only in groups two days a week.)

On September 7, 1977, the United States and Panama signed a new Panama Canal Treaty. When the treaty expires on December 31, 1999, Panama will have full charge of the Panama Canal for the first time in history.

Panama's national motto has been *Pro Mundi Beneficio*—For the Benefit of the World. When the canal becomes Panama's, will Panamanians still feel that way? Will they promote the best interests of all nations of the world? Will they selflessly preserve the ideal?

Or will they feel Panama's proper motto should be *Pro Panama Beneficio?* Will they try to use the canal to line Panamanians' pockets with gold?

An unsuccessful experiment tried to cut
costs by using a towing locomotive on
just one side of a ship. The rack
of twelve tires served as a rolling
bumper to hold the ship off the wall.

Chapter 8

WINDS OF
CHANGE

Omar Torrijos Herrera is widely revered in the hearts of Panamanians, who think of him as "Father of His Country."

Torrijos was an officer in the *Guardia Nacional*—the nation's army and police force—in 1968. The *Guardia Nacional* organized a coup d'etat and overthrew Panama's President Arnulfo Arias, and Torrijos emerged as leader of the group of ruling military officers, the junta.

In 1977, Torrijos and President Jimmy Carter signed the new Panama Canal Treaty that began transferring the canal from U.S. to Panamanian ownership. Panamanians said the nation divided by Theodore Roosevelt and the Panamanians of 1904 was reunited by Omar Torrijos.

Many Americans vigorously, vehemently, and vociferously opposed abandoning the old treaties that clearly gave the United States control over the Canal Zone "in perpetuity." They raised a ruckus that drew world attention.

Many Americans still do not understand why the President and Congress "gave away" America's canal.

The nature of the controversy surrounding the canal changed over the years. In the beginning, the principal debate raged around the question, "Can a canal be built?" There were so many doubters that President Roosevelt decided a canal would never be built unless he personally championed it:

. . . [T]he Panama Canal would not have been started if I had not taken hold of it, because if I had followed the traditional or conservative method

A joyful Omar Torrijos unexpectedly hugged President Jimmy Carter
before the ceremony to sign the 1977 Panama Canal treaties.

*I should have submitted an admirable state paper occupying a couple of
hundred pages detailing all of the facts to Congress and asking Congress'
consideration of it.*

*In that case there would have been a number of excellent speeches
made on the subject in Congress; the debate would be proceeding at this
moment [March 23, 1911] with great spirit and the beginning of work
on the canal would be fifty years in the future.*

*Fortunately the crisis came at a period when I could act unham-
pered. Accordingly I took the isthmus, started the canal and then left
Congress not to debate the canal, but to debate me.*[1]

In the middle years, there were Panamanian complaints that American
operation of the canal was unfair, but those complaints were largely over-
looked because the principal controversy was a different question: "Can
the canal be dramatically improved?"

The proposed dramatic improvement in 1931 was to build a third lane of locks next to the existing locks. When first opened, the canal could carry any ship afloat and every ship that asked. The locks were a roomy 1,000 feet long (305 m), 110 feet wide (33.5 m), with navigable depth of 40 feet (12.2 m). In the decade before 1931, the U.S. Navy asked for new locks to be added, locks 1,200 feet long (366 m), 140 feet wide (42.7 m), and 45 feet deep (13.7 m). They planned to build bigger battleships and aircraft carriers.

In 1931, doubters argued that the canal didn't have enough business to need a third lane of locks. The first ship in history built too large to transit the canal was Britain's *Queen Mary,* whose maiden voyage was not until 1936. And that ship was built to provide express passenger service between England and the United States. Its route across the North Atlantic meant it never would use the Panama Canal.

The Navy, to be sure, already had trouble with its aircraft carriers. Although their hulls fit into the locks, their flight decks were too wide and overlapped chamber walls. In March 1928, the U.S.S. *Lexington* was squeezing through when it slipped out of control and demolished six concrete lampposts and a handrail.

In 1939, Congress authorized construction of the third lane of larger locks. Digging began, but World War II caused all meaningful progress to stop.

By war's end, nuclear weapons gave doubters new ammunition. Navy officer Miles P. DuVal, Jr., a canal supervisor from 1941 to 1944, described the new twist: "In 1945 it was fear of the atomic bomb and other new weapon dangers that led to [new study of how to improve the canal and] recommendation in 1947 of only a canal of sea-level design for alleged reasons of 'security' and 'national defense.' "

The problem with any high-level lake canal was that one atomic blast could destroy it. Some people said a sea-level canal would be harder to damage and easier to repair. DuVal didn't agree. "As far as it has been possible to learn, leading authorities on nuclear warfare have uniformly held that any canal, regardless of type, is critically vulnerable to the atomic attack . . ."[2]

Later, debate favoring a sea-level canal ran up against new concerns about ecology. When the canal originally was constructed, no one studied how it would affect animal and plant life. In recent years, scientists discovered that Gatun Lake, because it is a very large body of fresh water, effectively isolates the Atlantic and Pacific oceans from one another. Flora and fauna able to live in the oceans' salt water usually are unable to

The *Lexington* out of control in Pedro Miguel Locks, just
after knocking over the first concrete lamppost

migrate from one ocean to the other, even if sticking to a ship's hull, because they cannot survive in the fresh water of Gatun Lake.

But a sea-level canal would let large amounts of salt water move between the oceans, carrying marine flora and fauna, with unknown consequences.

There are dangers. Pacific snails, starfish, and pufferfish might attack Caribbean coral reefs. The Eastern Pacific yellow-bellied snake might move into the Atlantic. The great barracuda and Portuguese man-of-war might move from the Atlantic to the Pacific.

Ecology does not favor all of the plans to add third locks to the high-level lake canal, either. Each transit dumps 52 million gallons (196.83 million l) of lake water through the locks to the sea. A third lane would use still more water. Existing lakes can't supply enough, and the simplest proposed solution to pump ocean water into Gatun Lake would change it to a salt lake, destroying the freshwater barrier.

Both third locks or sea-level design would be expensive. Politics discouraged Congress from investing any significant amount of money into building major, dramatic improvements.

When there was serious talk about building a sea-level canal, a witness told Congress, "We envisaged the construction of a sea-level canal as being so appealing to Panama that it would facilitate our continued operation of a canal on the Isthmus. We thought that Panama, in return for the huge investment in Panama, would give us the right to build and control a sea-level canal for a longer period than we could continue to control the lock canal."[3]

The Torrijos years sealed the decision. The overwhelming controversy became: "Can the canal continue to be American-owned?"

Torrijos said no.

By Torrijos's time, the world's other famous canal, the Suez, had been seized by its home nation, Egypt. When that happened, Great Britain and France began fighting a war to recapture "their property," but United States influence stopped them, leaving Egypt in full control.

When Torrijos became leader of Panama, he did not attempt military seizure of the canal; he did open peaceful negotiations with the United States to win turnover of the canal to Panama. But, at the same time, he had *Guardia Nacional* commandos trained to sabotage and close the canal and threatened guerrilla warfare.

The president and Congress decided to peacefully deliver the canal to Panama over a transition period of twenty years.

Seal of the Panama Canal Commission

By 1977, U.S. interest in the canal was less overwhelming than it had been in 1904. Trucks and trains carried much of the freight coast to coast within the United States. Aircraft carried both mail and passengers. Americans in 1904 associated ships with international travel. Americans in 1977 thought first of airplanes. America no longer was primarily a seafaring nation; it had become an aviation nation instead.

Politically, the United States no longer dominated the western hemisphere the way it did in 1904. Feelings of people in the United States and elsewhere had changed. Third World nations had new power created largely by the increased speed of communications, by development of international journalism, and by development of new feelings about human rights and national interests. For the United States to even appear to force its will on nations of the western hemisphere today raises charges of imperialism and antagonizes America's neighbor nations.

The world had changed since 1904.

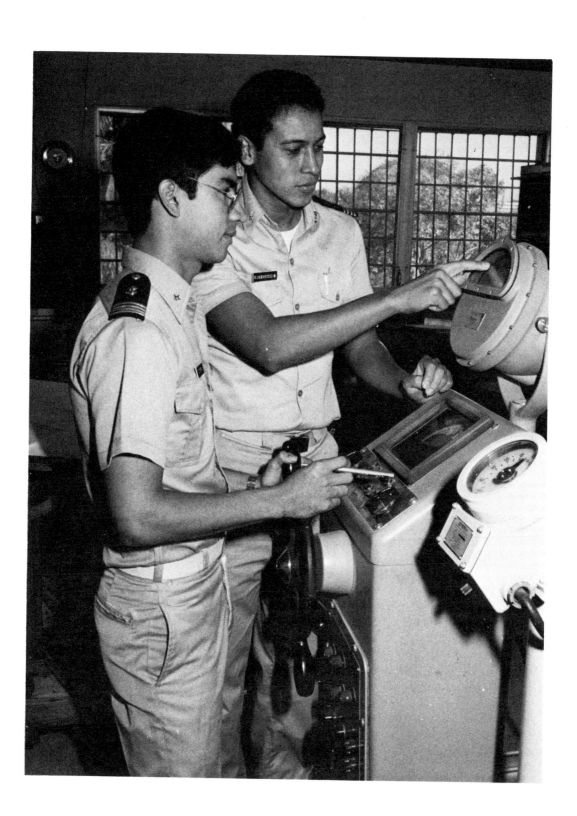

In 1978 Senator Mike Gravel stated his view of the new political reality:

If . . . it is on Panamanian soil, or Nicaraguan soil, or Bolivian soil, you better believe that it is going to be a Panamanian Canal, it is going to be a Nicaraguan Canal or Bolivian Canal, and anyone that thinks it is going to be otherwise has not arrived into the 20th century.[4]

Since 1973, students from the Panama Nautical School have trained aboard Panama Canal launches, tugboats, and dredges. Upon graduation, they qualify to be engineers and mates aboard Panamanian merchant ships.

APPENDIX

The Panama Canal is 50 miles (80.5 km) long from deep water in the Atlantic to deep water in the Pacific. It was cut through one of the narrowest places and at one of the lowest saddles of the long isthmus that joins the North and South American continents. The saddle originally was 340 feet (103.6 m) above sea level where it crosses the Continental Divide in the rugged mountain range.

The canal runs from northwest to southeast with the Atlantic entrance being 33.5 miles (55.5 km) north and 27 miles (43.5 km) west of the Pacific entrance. The airline distance between the two entrances is 43 miles (69.2 km).

Principal physical features of the canal are the two terminal ports, short sections of the channel at either end at sea level, the three sets of twin locks, Gatun Lake and Gaillard (formerly Culebra) Cut.

The sea-level section of the canal on the Atlantic side is 6.5 miles (10.5 km) long. This section of the channel is 500 feet (152.4 m) wide and runs through a mangrove swamp that is only a few feet above sea level in most places.

It requires about eight or nine hours for an average ship to transit the canal. A ship is raised or lowered a total of 85 feet (26 m) in a continuous flight of three steps at Gatun Locks. Each lock chamber is 110 feet (33.5 m) wide and 1,000 feet (305 m) long. The length of Gatun Locks, including the two approach walls, is 1.2 miles (1.92 km).

Gatun Lake, through which the ships travel for 23.5 miles (37.8 km) from Gatun Locks to the north end of Gaillard Cut, is one of the largest

Low tide exposes mud flats to reveal the narrow channel and
dangerous hidden banks at the canal's Pacific entrance. Compare
this to the picture on page 56 that shows the area at high tide.

Battleship USS *New Jersey* southbound through Pedro Miguel Locks, June 1968

Pegasus enters Miraflores Locks at the beginning of its historic transit

artificial bodies of water in the world. It covers an area of 164 square miles (423.1 square km) and was formed by an earthen dam across the Chagres River adjacent to Gatun Locks. The two wings of the dam and the spillway have a total length of about 1.5 miles (2.4 km). The dam is nearly a half-mile (.8 km) wide at the base, sloping to a width of 100 feet (30.5 m) at the crest, which is 105 feet (32 m) above sea level, or 20 feet (6.1 m) above the normal level of Gatun Lake.

Gaillard Cut was called Culebra Cut during the construction period and later was renamed to honor David DuBose Gaillard, the engineer who was in charge of this section of the canal work. This 9-mile-long (14.5 km) portion of the channel cuts through rock and shale for most of the distance. It was here that the principal excavation was required and here that major landslides occurred during construction and soon after the canal was opened.

The Pacific-bound ship enters Pedro Miguel Locks at the south end of Gaillard Cut. Here it is lowered 31 feet (9.5 m) in one step to Miraflores Lake, a small artificial body of water 1.88 square miles (4.8 square km) that separates the two sets of Pacific locks. The length of Pedro Miguel Locks is five-sixths of a mile (1.33 km).

The transiting ship is lowered the remaining two steps to sea level at Miraflores Locks, which are slightly over a mile in length. The lock gates at Miraflores are the highest of any in the system because of the extreme tidal variation (more than 20 feet [6.1 m]) in the Pacific Ocean.

SOURCE NOTES

Chapter 1

1. "Gianelli Stands Behind Panamanian Employees," *The Panama Canal Spillway*. Balboa, Panama, Dec. 2, 1988, p. 1; "Commission Adopts Package to Aid Victims of Tax Proceedings," *The Panama Canal Spillway*, Jan. 13, 1989, p. 1; Letter, Ambassador Arthur H. Davis, *The Panama Canal Spillway*, Jan 13, 1989, p. 1.
2. Personal communication to the author.
3. "Fiftieth Anniversary Supplement," *The Panama Canal Review*. Balboa Heights, Panama Canal Zone, May 4, 1954, p. 4.
4. Condensed and edited from Ferdinand de Lesseps, *Recollections of Forty Years*, trans. by C. B. Pitman. London: Chapman and Hall, 1887, vol. 2, p. 188.
5. Interoceanic Canal Congress, "Report of Final General Session, May 29, 1879," in *Compte Rendu des Seances*. Paris, 1879, p. 651.
6. De Lesseps, p. 200.
7. "New Republic May Arise to Grant Canal," *New York World*, June 14, 1903, p. 4.

Chapter 2

1. U.S. reconnaissance located the Spanish Caribbean fleet in Santiago harbor, where it arrived on May 19, just ahead of the *Oregon*. U.S. ships, including the *Oregon*, blockaded the harbor entrance while U.S. troops landed to the east and marched toward the harbor. To escape capture, the Spanish admiral led his ships to sea on July 3 and engaged the American naval vessels in battle. All Spanish ships received severe damage and were beached.
2. "Centuries Spent on Surveys and Plans for Canals on Main Isthmian Routes," *The Panama Canal Review*, March 1, 1957, p. 10.
3. Extract from von Humboldt's *Political Essay on the Kingdom of New Spain*, in U.S. Congress, House, "Canal or Railroad Between the Atlantic and Pacific Oceans," February 20, 1849, p. 179.

4. Sample in Manuscript Division, Library of Congress. See also Philippe Bunau-Varilla, *Panama: The Creation, Destruction, and Resurrection.* New York: McBride, Nast, 1914, pp. 246–247.

5. U.S. Congress, Senate, Committee on Foreign Relations, *Background Documents Relating to the Panama Canal.* Washington: Government Printing Office, 1977, p. 710.

6. National Assembly of Panama, Document 67 in U.S. House of Representatives, 66th Congress, 1st Session. In the original translation, ''Panamanian'' is spelled ''Panaman.''

Chapter 3

1. *Annual Report of the Governor of the Panama Canal, 1943*, p. 70.

2. Earl Harding, *The Untold Story of Panama.* New York: Athene Press, 1959, p. 159.

3. Theodore Roosevelt, *An Autobiography.* New York: Macmillan, 1913, p. 543.

4. LeCurrieux and other workers quoted in this chapter wrote contest essays. See Isthmian Historical Society, ''Competition for the Best True Stories of Life and Work on the Isthmus of Panama During the Construction of the Panama Canal.'' Balboa Heights, Panama Canal Zone, unpublished, 1963. Excerpts condensed and edited.

Chapter 4

1. The *Aedes aegypti* was known in Major Reed's time as the *Stegomyia fasciata.*

2. U.S. Congress, House, Committee on Interstate and Foreign Commerce, *Hearings on the Isthmian Canal, June 5, 1906.* Washington, D.C.: Government Printing Office, 1906, pp. 13–14.

3. Ibid, pp. 16–17.

4. William L. Sibert and John F. Stevens, *The Construction of the Panama Canal.* New York: D. Appleton, 1915, pp. 90–91.

5. Ibid, p. 90.

6. Joseph Bucklin Bishop and Farnham Bishop, *Goethals: Genius of the Panama Canal.* New York: Harper, 1930, p. 143.

7. Mark Sullivan, *Our Times: The United States 1900–1925.* New York: Scribner's, 1937, vol. 1, p. 466.

8. Arthur Bullard, ''Court of Low, Middle, and High Justice,'' *The Panama Canal Review,* April 2, 1954, p. 12. Previously published in Albert Edwards (pseud), *Panama: The Canal, the Country and the People.* New York: Macmillan, 1911, pp. 503–504.

9. Bishop and Bishop, p. 209.

Chapter 5

1. ''Memorial to George W. Goethals Compiled on Behalf of His Canal Associates and Friends, 1928,'' unpublished scrapbook.

2. Bishop and Bishop, pp. 261–262.

3. Ibid, p. 263.

4. Ibid, p. 264.

5. "Memorial to George W. Goethals . . ."

6. *Official Handbook of the Panama Canal*. Washington, D. C.: Government Printing Office, 1915, p. 33.

7. Jay J. Morrow, *The Maintenance and Operation of The Panama Canal*. Mount Hope, Panama Canal Zone: Panama Canal Press, 1923, p. 9.

8. R. J. Alfaro, "Well-Deserved Tribute," *The Panama Canal Review,* October 5, 1962, p. 6.

Chapter 6

1. W. A. Card, Letter to U.S. Department of Commerce Steamboat Inspection Service, New Orleans, La., dated November 7, 1923.

2. Quoted in Julius Grigore, Jr., "The O-5 Is Down!" *U.S. Naval Institute Proceedings,* February 1972, p. 58.

3. "Submarine O-5 Sunk in Cristobal Harbor," *Star and Herald,* Panama City, Panama, October 29, 1923.

4. Rodney R. Robertson, "The Holocaust at Coal Hoist Bend." *Safety at Sea,* Surrey, England, June 1974, p. 9. Reprinted by permission. Omits final paragraphs assigning blame to "officials" acting over protests of Panama Canal Pilots' Association.

5. Often misreported as one hundred holes on the chamber floor. In fact, the lower chambers at Miraflores Locks, and the lower and middle chambers at Gatun Locks, have ten lateral culverts connecting from the centerwall culvert and eleven laterals from the sidewall culvert, each supplying five holes on the chamber floor. All other lock chambers have a twelfth culvert from the sidewall that supplies an additional nine holes in the space between the two sets of miter gates at the downstream end of the chamber.

6. Richard Halliburton, *New Worlds to Conquer*. Indianapolis, Ind.: Bobbs-Merrill, 1929, p. 116.

Chapter 7

1. *Official Handbook of the Panama Canal*. Washington, D.C.: Government Printing Office, 1915, p. 32.

2. Stanford Research Institute, "Panama Canal Tolls," *SRI Journal*. Menlo Park, Calif., November 1967, p. 11.

Chapter 8

1. *San Francisco Examiner,* March 24, 1911, p. 2.

2. U.S. Congress, House, Committee on Merchant Marine and Fisheries, *Hearings Before the Subcommittee on the Panama Canal, June 21, 27, 28, 1978*. Washington, D.C.: Government Printing Office, 1978, p. 481.

3. Ibid, p. 315.

4. U.S. Congress, House, Committee on Merchant Marine and Fisheries, *Hearings Before the Subcommittee on the Panama Canal, June 21, 27, 28, 1978*. Washington, D.C.: Government Printing Office, 1978, p. 42.

BIBLIOGRAPHY

Bishop, Joseph Bucklin, and Farnham Bishop. *Goethals: Genius of the Panama Canal.* New York: Harper, 1930. Biography of the chief engineer who finished canal construction, with events leading up to Opening Day. Authors were on-scene.

Duval, Miles P., Jr. *And the Mountains Will Move.* Stanford, Calif.: Stanford University Press, 1947. Construction days and operation of the canal during early years. Researched while author was working as a senior canal official.

Hlavecek, Lawrence L. *The Isthmian Canal.* Wellesley Hills, Mass.: Independent School Press, 1969. A source book—reprints of original reports and treaties.

McCain, William D. *The United States and the Republic of Panama.* New York: Russell & Russell, 1965 reissue of 1937 Duke University Press original. Sovereignty—the events and arguments of the major dispute that began in 1903.

McCullough, David. *The Path Between the Seas: The Creation of the Panama Canal 1870–1914.* New York: Simon & Schuster, 1977. Construction days and the lives of key people—history told as adventure.

Ryan, Paul B. *The Panama Canal Controversy.* Stanford, Calif.: Hoover Institution Press, 1977. Political controversies, especially in recent years.

Sibert, William L., and John F. Stevens. *The Construction of the Panama Canal.* New York: D. Appleton, 1915. Two men who built the canal tell how.

Small, Charles S. *Rails to the Diggings: Construction Railroads of the Panama Canal.* Cos Cob, Conn.: Charles S. Small, 11 Dandy Drive, 1981. Railroads were vital to construction—an experienced railroad man tells how; many photographs.

Stevens, John F. *An Engineer's Recollections.* New York: McGraw-Hill, 1936. Designing the canal and the work force—Stevens won recognition for doing both.

Vinton, Kenneth W. *The Jungle Whispers.* New York: Pageant Press, 1956. Snakes, crocodiles, cayman, and other creatures that live near the canal.

INDEX

Alternate shipping routes, 72, 75, 83
Amador, Manuel, 24–25
Arias, Arnulfo, 78

Balboa, Vasco Nunez de, 13
Bierd, William G., 41
Breault, Henry, 62
Brown, Lawrence, 62
Bullard, Arthur, 44
Bunau-Varilla, Philippe, 23, 25

Card, W. A., 58–60
Carmichael, Leslie, 28
Carter, Jimmy, 78
Charles V, king of Spain, 13
Colombia, 16, 21
Columbus, Christopher, 13
Construction of Panama Canal, 13, 26–35, 36–47
Cuba, 11, 12, 19–21, 36

De Lepinay, Adolphe Godin, 38
De Lesseps, Ferdinand, 14
Dingler, Jules Isadore, 15–16, 36
DuVal, Miles P., Jr., 80

Ecological concerns, 80–82
Egypt, 82

Emergencies, handling of, 58–71

Financial viability of Panama Canal, 11, 54, 72–77
France, 13, 14–16, 38

Gianelli, William R., 12
Goethals, George Washington, 44–47, 48–50
Gorgas, William Crawford, 26, 36
Gravel, Mike, 85
Grenada, 11

Halliburton, Richard, 68
Harding, Earl, 26
Health and construction of Panama Canal, 26, 36–37
Herran, Tomas, 16
Hodges, George, 33–34
Holocaust at Coal Hoist Bend, 62–64

Improvements to Panama Canal, proposed, 79–82

Kennedy, John F., 12
Kirkby, Tim, 65

LeCurrieux, J. E., 28

Lewis, James A., 34–35

McKeen, John, 69
Malaria, 37, 57
Morgan, John Tyler, 22
Morrow, Jay J., 54

New York World, 16–17, 26
Nicaragua, 11, 22, 23
Noriega, Manuel Antonio, 12

Opening of Panama Canal, 48–50
Operations, Panama Canal, 58–71
Ownership, Panama Canal, 10–11, 77, 78, 82–85

Panama, independence of, 16–18, 23–25
Panama Canal:
    construction of, 13, 26–35, 36–47
    financial viability of, 11, 54, 72–77
    opening of, 48–50
    operations, 58–71
    ownership of, 10–11, 77, 78, 82–85
    physical features, 86–89
    proposed improvements, 79–82
    route of, 22–23, 38–39
Panama Canal Treaty (1903), 23–25, 57 (1977), 77, 78
Panama Canal Zone, 23, 24, 25, 48, 52
Panama/United States relations, 9–13, 16–18, 48, 52–53, 57, 58, 79, 82–85
    See also Panama Canal Treaty
Peters, Albert, 30–31
Physical features of Panama Canal, 86–89

Porras, Belisario, 48
Public health and construction of canal, 26, 36–37

Racial discrimination and construction of Panama Canal, 26
Reed, Walter, 36
Robertson, Rodney, 62–65
Rodman, Hugh, 50
Roosevelt, Theodore, 22, 24, 28, 36, 39, 41–44, 78–79
Route of Panama Canal, 22–23, 38–39

Saville, C. M., 48
Shreaves, Shep, 58, 60–62
Simmons, Edgar Llewellyn, 28–30
Spain, 13–14, 19–21
SRI International, 72–75
Star & Herald, 61
Stevens, John Frank, 36, 37–41
Suez Canal, 82
Superships, 72, 75

Tobar, Juan, 17
Tolls, Panama Canal, 72–77
Torrijos, Omar, 78, 82

United States/Panama relations, 9–13, 16–18, 48, 52–53, 57, 58, 79, 82–85
    See also Panama Canal Treaty

Von Humboldt, Alexander, 21

Williams, James A., 31–33

Yellow fever, 36, 37, 57

ABOUT
THE AUTHOR

Carl Oliver lived on a hillside overlooking the Panama Canal for nearly two years while researching this book. He rode ships through the canal, talked to canal pilots, and, with the help of canal employees, found historic documents in both Panama and Washington, D.C.

Panama's Canal grew out of his observation that Americans visiting the canal knew a little about *what* the canal is and *who* built it, but hardly anything about the *whys* and *hows* of its psychosocial, economic, and political environment.

Carl Oliver was born in Ft. Lewis, Washington. He graduated from Stanford University with a degree in psychology and earned an M.B.A. from California Lutheran University. His experience as a commissioned officer in the Air Force, including three years teaching aerospace studies at Stanford, led to his first book, *Plane Talk,* in which famous aviators described the thrill of flying.

Mr. Oliver currently lives in Thousand Oaks, California, and coaches employees of an aircraft manufacturer on practical ways to improve the quality of their work and the quality of the firm's products.